Death Among Friends

Elizabeth Cadell

The Friendly Air Publishing

thefriendlyairpublishing.com

Chapter One

My instructions were specific. I was to meet the Cornish Express at 12:40, collect James Lubin Maitland and his luggage and drive him to his aunt's house in Cranston Avenue, arriving in good time for lunch. Nothing, Madame had said, could be simpler.

She had said it that morning, sitting up in bed with her breakfast tray before her. Around her, as usual, was a mess of torn envelopes from the morning's letters, scattered toast crumbs and spilt sugar. Across her vast bosom, bursting from its faded pink jacket, were moist circular coffee stains; some of them, spilt directly below the safety-pins that she used to reinforce the buttons of her jacket, looked like erratically-placed medals.

"It is quite simple. You will drive to the station. James will come at twenty minutes to one. Tell the cook that we shall have the lamb chops for lunch."

I had written a few letters for her, taken them upstairs for her to sign, run her bath, shouted instructions for lunch down the speaking-tube to the cook in her subterranean quarters, put a set of towels into the room allocated to James Lubin Maitland, and then set off to the station.

I wasn't surprised, when I got there, to find that the 12:40 wasn't the Cornish Express and that Madame's nephew, James Maitland, wasn't on it. Madame's time-tables were always worked out in great detail, but her trains had either ceased to run or were running on a changed schedule; her guests weren't coming this week, but next. Ships and planes invariably foxed her by coming and going when they said they would, and not when she thought they would.

I went to a phone booth, rang her up and told her that the Cornish Express was to arrive not at 12:40 but at 2:20, and that if her nephew was travelling on it he would in all probability have lunched in the restaurant-car. I myself, I told her, would fill in the period of waiting by having sandwiches and coffee in the station buffet.

"In that case," she said, "I shall order for myself an omelette. The lamb chops will be for dinner."

As always when I heard her deep, rich, heavily accented voice on the phone, I felt that she was beside me in person; I could see her big, red face, her shapely arms, her quivering chins and dry, grey, naturally frizzy hair.

"But Alison, my dear, you are sure about this 2:20?" she shouted anxiously. "You have not mistaken?"

"No, Madame."

"I have lost James's letter, but I am so sure that he said 1:20, or perhaps he said 1:30. He is so careless, poor boy, his head is up in the clouds. Why will you not come home and eat something here? The station is so dirty."

"There isn't time to go back to lunch," I said.

"Then go and eat something to nourish you. You are too thin. Have meat and potatoes and some good pudding."

I said that I would nourish myself adequately, and rang off. I went to the refreshment-room and sat at a table near the window; I ordered cheese and coffee and stared out at the hurrying crowds. I felt chilly, and longed to be outside in the spring sunshine; I liked trains, but loathed railway stations with their bleak platforms, bewildering noise and general grimness.

I bought a paper from a newsboy and opened it idly. The latest rocket was still in orbit; the Queen was in Wales and the dockers were back at work. There was a photograph of pilgrims setting off to Fatima for the May 13th celebrations, and a strip cartoon showing a lightly-clad girl holding off a man who had mistaken her for what she was.

I put down the paper and looked at my watch. Two o'clock; only twenty minutes to go. I turned and signalled for my bill; when I turned back, one man out of the many passing the window caught and held my gaze.

I sat motionless and watched him walking slowly out of sight. When he had gone, I still sat unmoving, staring out at a scene that was no longer a station. Then I saw him walking back again—walking on to the scene as he had walked on to it eighteen months ago. Easily, gracefully, negligently...

7

I heard a sound and looked down to see the newspaper shaking violently in my clenched hands. With a desperate effort I got myself under control and then put things slowly back into perspective. Neil Patterson was out there, either waiting—like myself—to meet someone, or waiting for his own train; there were several million faces in London; there was no need to become hysterical on recognising one among them.

He was walking slowly up and down, passing and repassing the window. My bill came and I paid it and sat on hoping he'd move away—but he didn't. To and fro, back and forth, steady and unhurried...

Two-eighteen. I chose a moment when his back was turned. I went swiftly to the door, took two steps and came face to face with him.

I had nothing to say. Nor, for some moments, had he. We stood staring at one another and I saw the first instant's shock, and then the narrowed eyes taking me in, searching, probing, assessing.

He was unchanged, I thought. There was the same slim, tallish figure, the same lean, dark face, the long nose, the black, gleaming eyes. My earliest impressions of him had been that he looked like a devil. I had learned that the resemblance was more than skin deep.

He spoke at last, in the brusque way I remembered.

"Odd. London was the one place in which I never dreamt of looking."

A luggage wagon separated us for a few moments. When it had passed, I saw that he was frowning.

"What made you come so far from your native heath?" he asked.

"You," I said.

He smiled, and I remembered how surprised I had been the first time I saw that transfiguration.

"Have you been in London all the time?"

"Yes," I said.

"Eighteen months is quite a time."

"Eighteen months and four days."

There was a pause.

"I was in Edinburgh three weeks ago. I went to see your godmother," he said. "You should have told her where you were."

"I did tell her where I was."

"She said she hadn't had a line from you since you left."

I was going to say that she had lied, but I couldn't imagine her lying, so I said nothing.

"Are you happy?" he asked suddenly.

"Yes," I said.

"I'm glad. Working?"

"Yes."

"Where?"

"Does it matter to you?"

9

"I worried like hell about you."

"Why?"

"Because—" He stopped.

"You shouldn't let things lie on your conscience," I said evenly. "And now, if you'll excuse me, I've got to meet somebody."

"So have I," he said. "Platform 10."

We moved towards it together. There was no train standing there. Looking up at the Arrivals board, we learned that the Cornish Express was seven minutes late.

"Strange coincidence," remarked Neil, "to meet again meeting the same train after eighteen months."

"And four days."

He stared at me for some moments.

"You've changed," he said.

"In some ways," I agreed. "Thanks to you."

We were standing by the barrier and my hand was on one of the railings. He put his own on it.

"Look, Alison," he said, "I'm sorry about what happened."

"I was too," I said. "But not any more."

I drew my hand away and we stood in silence. Neil's face lost its fleeting look of gentleness and took on the habitual brooding expression I knew so well. The train came in at last, slowly and smoothly.

"I suppose," he said, "it's no good asking for your address?"

"No use at all."

"Then will you write to your godmother?"

"I did write to her. I told you. I wrote twice, but I got no reply."

"One of you—you or she—has missed a trick somewhere," he said.

I made no answer. I was looking at the people streaming out of the train. I knew more or less what I was looking for—a man of thirty-two, tall and lean, with untidy hair and a faraway expression. Madame had no likeness of him taken after the age of thirteen, but during the past few months his photographs had appeared frequently in the papers—leaving Norway, arriving in Paris, attending the first performance of the Lubin play, leaving Paris, arriving at his cottage in Cornwall.

It was not until most of the passengers had passed through the barrier that I caught sight of him. Neil had obviously been following my glance, and I heard his amazed question.

"You're not by any extraordinary chance meeting James Maitland?"

"Yes, I am."

"You know him?"

"Not yet. I work for his aunt."

"Is she an actress?"

I said that she wasn't, and didn't add that she was more theatrical than anybody on any stage.

11

"What do you want with him?" I asked.

"Don't you read the papers? I'm producing his uncle's play—the Lubin play. It's being given its first performance at the Edinburgh Festival in August. I tried to see him when I was going through Paris on my way to Italy, but I missed him. When I got back to England yesterday, I tried to get him in Cornwall, and missed him again. I rang up this morning and heard that he was coming in on the Cornish Express. I'm not in the habit of running after playwrights, but I've got to talk to him. Is he going to stay with this aunt of his?"

"Yes."

"I'd like her address."

There was no point in withholding it. He noted it down.

James Maitland had almost reached us. The nearer he got, the longer he looked. Everything about him was long—too long. His hair was too long. His legs and arms were too long. His jacket was too long. His trousers were so long that for one uneasy moment I thought they were falling down. The faraway expression turned out to be merely a preoccupied air. He knew he was being met, because Madame had telephoned to tell him so, but he showed no interest whatsoever in the people waiting at the barrier. He approached with long, leisurely strides, his eyes looking straight ahead; he would have walked straight past us if Neil and I hadn't spoken together.

"Mr. Maitland."

He stopped and gazed at us as though he was trying to get

us into focus.

"Yes?"

Neil gave me no time to say anything.

"My name's Patterson." His manner, as always, was curt and unsmiling. "I wrote to you several times."

"Ah," said James Maitland.

"This is Miss Sinclair, who works for your aunt."

"Ah," said Mr. Maitland.

"She's given me your aunt's address. I'll get in touch with you there."

"Ah," said James Maitland.

He said it reflectively. He was taking us both in. His eyes were calm and grey, with lashes that on an actress would have been labelled smoky. He looked younger than his thirty-two years. He was carrying nothing more than a briefcase.

'Is your luggage in the van?" I asked.

"No. Porter." He indicated the porter waiting close by.

"Then let's go," I said.

Neil turned to me and spoke abruptly.

"Perhaps you're going to decide to disappear for another year and a half, leaving no trace," he said. "Before you go, perhaps you can get through to Mr. Maitland the fact that a number of busy members of the theatrical profession would like his attention."

He turned on his heel and walked away. James Maitland looked after him with mild astonishment and the faint dawning of dislike. I began to warm towards him.

"Friend of yours ?" he inquired.

"No. Shall we go? I've got your aunt's car here."

He followed me and the porter followed him. I led the way to Madame's ancient but capacious car, and the porter strapped the suitcases on to the luggage grid while James Maitland fumbled for coins. He paid the porter and I was about to walk round and take my place at the wheel when without any warning he looked wildly towards the luggage and gave a loud cry.

"Wait!" he shouted, and turning, went swiftly towards the platform we had just left. Checked by an official at the barrier, he swerved and pushed through the throng making their way on to the adjacent platform. Brushing past a protesting ticket collector, he made for the recently-arrived Cornish Express. Dodging trucks, leaping over mail bags, he went almost the length of the train before vanishing into a carriage near the rear.

I waited, reminding myself that he was, after all, related to Madame; he was bound to have some peculiarities.

I saw him reappear and face the knot of officials who had gathered to ask him what he thought he was doing. He was clutching an outsized umbrella, and I saw him hold it out while the officials closed round it and peered at it with interest. Then they parted and made way for him, and he came back to join me. He had regained his calm and unhurried air.

"Nearly left my umbrella behind," he explained. "That's

the fourth time. Twice in Paris, once in Cornwall and now here."

"There's a left-luggage office," I pointed out. "You'd probably have got it back."

"This isn't just an umbrella," he explained, a touch of frost in his voice. "This was given to me by the people of Transel."

Transel, I knew, was the small Norwegian town in which his uncle, Olav Lubin, had lived and died.

He held out the umbrella and indicated the little silver plaque attached to its handle.

"My name, and a message. Look."

I looked. The message, being written in Norwegian, meant nothing to me.

"Good wishes for a good trip?" I hazarded.

"You don't quite understand," he said, displeased. "They gave me this umbrella as a memento of the time I spent in Transel. They chose an umbrella because they believed England to be a rainy country. I have been photographed a good deal recently, and the photographs have appeared in the Norwegian Press. In every photograph I have been holding the umbrella, open or shut according to the weather. In all photographs—outdoor photographs—I want to have the umbrella with me to show that I appreciate the gift."

"It'll usually be open," I said. "We're having a wet spring."

We said nothing more until I had driven some way from the station. Then he asked me how Madame was.

"She's very well. She would have come herself, but she had to arrange some classes."

"She still holds those classes?"

"Yes."

"And still gets pupils?" he marvelled.

"There's a waiting list."

"Have you been with her long?"

"Seventeen months. Her last secretary got married."

"They used to come and go," he commented. "They were always young and good-looking and they never lasted long. Seventeen months seems an unusually long time."

I didn't tell him that it had seemed a very short time to me. I didn't tell him that the seventeen months had been refuge and healing and interest and fascination, in that order. I didn't tell him anything.

"It's some time since you've seen her, isn't it?" I asked.

"I was about fourteen. She terrified me. I expected her to be like her brother in Transel, or like my mother, who was her sister—but Madame wasn't like anybody I'd ever seen before. I thought for the first few days that she was off her head. She acted like a... Well, she just acted."

In that respect, I mused, he wouldn't find her much changed. It had taken me a long time to believe that she had never appeared professionally.

James Maitland was looking at the passing scene. We were skirting Buckingham Palace and he glanced up at the empty flagpole.

"Nobody at home," he said.

"No."

"All these houses"—he waved a hand—"used to fascinate me. Belgravia. Carriages and coachmen and pampered, expensively-gowned women. And now buses and busy housewives."

I drove up Cranston Avenue and stopped before the shabby but imposing entrance of Number 18. James Maitland sat still, studying it.

"I've never understood how she's managed to keep it on," he commented, half to himself. "Almost every other house in the street turned into flats or shops or rooms-to-let, but this one intact. Where does the money come from?"

I had my own ideas, but I didn't pass them on. He got out and was walking up the steps carrying his umbrella when I called him back.

"I'm afraid you'll have to carry up your own luggage," I told him. "There's a series of daily women, but they don't fetch and they won't carry."

He assembled the suitcases on the pavement. He handed me the brief-case and I handed it back again.

"I'll take the umbrella," I said.

We went inside, Maitland panting under his load. There was nobody to greet us. The door of what Madame called the reception-room was closed, and behind it one of her classes was in progress. James Maitland and I, standing in the large, bare hall with his luggage at our feet, could hear her admonishing her pupils; we could both picture her on her low platform at one end of the room, dressed in her flowing black tunic, her beautiful arms bare, her imperial figure swaying. Her pupils were all women, ranging in age from twenty-five to forty-five. A gramophone with a long- playing record was playing waltzes.

"One—two—three, down, up, turn, down, up, turn, one, two, three... The lady in row three," Madame requested, "please to do this alone. Down, please. Down. One, two, three—Ah, that is better! All together. One, two, three; one. . ."

When Madame had first interviewed me, she had said nothing about her Norwegian Drill classes. Not having seen the secretary who preceded me, I had had no opportunity of getting any information on the side. Madame herself seemed to think that I would know everything intuitively. One by one, facts and details emerged; when at last Madame told me about the Norwegian Drill, I had felt acutely embarrassed— she couldn't, I decided, mean that she actually conducted the classes herself. Who would dream of taking slimming instruction from this mountain of a woman? It wasn't until I saw her on the platform that I understood why there were always pupils eager to be enrolled. I'm not given to thinking in picturesque terms, but her movements made me think of the sea—the sea in a gentle swell, rising and falling rhythmically, languorously, its force and power for the moment lulled.

James Maitland was wandering round the hall, opening doors and peering into rooms. They were all large and cold. The furniture was heavy, the curtains and carpets faded to a uniform grey. The chair covers were of patched chintz or tattered brocade through which the stuffing was escaping. The walls of the dining-room were hung with mirrors, which made eating a somewhat self-conscious process.

"You've tidied it up," he remarked at the end of his inspection. "You or somebody else."

I took him, luggage-laden, up to his room and left him to settle in. When he came downstairs, I was wheeling the teathings into the drawing-room.

"Is the Norwegian cook—the one called Aud—still here?" he asked.

"Yes."

"I'll go down and see her."

He went away, and I reflected that—unlike Neil Patterson—he could be abrupt without seeming discourteous. Before he returned, I heard the bustle that denoted the end of the class, and went into the hall to see the pupils off the premises. As the last one left, Madame, a long cloak thrown over her tunic, came hurrying out of the reception-room, and at the same moment James Maitland appeared at the bend of the staircase leading from the basement. Her arms held wide to embrace him, Madame advanced, her face alight with welcome. Before he could reach the top and take evasive action, his head was seized and pressed against her billowing bosom and held fast while she recited a speech in Norwegian. Then she released him and turned to address me in English.

"Tea, Alison, tea!" she cried.

She led him into the room and then held him at arms' length to study him.

"Too thin," she announced. "You have been working too hard, James—but you have grown so much more like your uncle." She sank into a chair and sighed heavily. "Ah, my poor Olav! So many years of work unrecognised, and then at the last, honour and esteem—but still poverty. It is strange that you are to grow rich on his work—but I am glad for you. Sit down, sit down, James, and talk to me. Tell me everything, from the moment that you went to Norway. Everything."

They talked and I listened. James Maitland took great hot gulps of tea and large bites of buttered toast, from time to time holding out his cup or his plate for refilling. Between the lean, tall man and the enormous woman I was surprised to detect certain likenesses—their wide-set grey eyes, their short noses, their complete lack of self-consciousness. They seemed to have forgotten that I was present; their talk was of their family in general and the late Olav Lubin in particular. I listened with interest; some of it I knew already, but much of it was new.

Success had touched Madame's brother too late. He died in his native town of Transel in Norway esteemed by his countrymen and by a limited international following, but with little material gain to show for his forty years of literary work. Without wife or heirs, he left his papers unconditionally to his nephew, son of his sister and her English husband. James Maitland, then himself a struggling playwright, was living in a cottage in Cornwall; he sent his widowed mother back to her native Norway, and until her death she had occupied her late brother's house and kept guard over his papers. Going to Norway to attend her funeral, James Maitland had had no other plan in mind but to sell the house in Transel and return to England. Far from returning, he had lived there for the past three years, caught fast in the fascination of discovering for the first time the quality of his uncle's work. His first translation, to his own surprise, had been made into French, and the play had recently been performed with notable success in Paris. A second play, translated into English, was in James Maitland's bulky brief-case—and that was where Neil Patterson came in.

The voices in the room seemed to grow fainter. I was back for a moment where Neil Patterson had that morning told me I belonged—in Scotland. I was back in the house in which I had been brought up—my godmother's house. I was sitting by the fire; then, as now, beside a tea-table, looking at a man who had just entered the room. I don't know why so many Scots are credited with so much second sight; apart from registering that the years had made him look even more sinister, I can't pretend that I had any premonition whatsoever.

I came back to the present to see Madame on her way out of the drawing room; she was going upstairs to rest before taking her second class from five to six o'clock. I heard James Maitland addressing me, half in apology.

"Madame and I talked a lot," he said.

"You had a lot to talk about."

He sat down again and stared at me absently across the room.

"She's changed," he said.

"Or you have."

"I suppose that's it. All the same, I can see why I was frightened. I was a very *small* little boy. In those days, I thought of her as immensely rich—this house was so much grander than our own. What's happened to the furniture? The place used to be stuffed."

"I don't know," I said.

It was true. I didn't know what had happened to it; I could only guess. Items were carried away from time to time by workmen in overalls; some pieces came back, others didn't.

"I suppose it never occurred to my mother or to my uncle that Madame wasn't as rich as she claimed to be. She was regarded as the prosperous one of the family. My uncle's works brought in very little while he was alive; her sister—my mother—married an absent-minded country solicitor who seldom got around to collecting his bills. He couldn't bear Madame."

"Why do you always address her as Madame?" I asked.

"It was the only name I ever heard her called in the family. Her name's Norma, but I never heard anybody use it."

"Not even your mother?"

"Not even my mother. My mother simply referred to her

22

as Madame. She used to come up to London now and again and spend a few days in this house, but my father would never come with her. He had a rather rigid code of behaviour, and Madame operated outside it."

"Why was she called Madame in the first place? Did she marry a Frenchman?"

"She didn't marry anybody. She left home with a Polish count and left him—it's said—for an English diplomat. It must have been the English diplomat who bought her this house; she certainly owns it. She kept the name Lubin because she was proud of it. So was my mother; that's why she gave it to me. Do you have anything to do with Madame's financial affairs?"

"She gives two lessons a day on Mondays and Fridays," I replied. "On Mondays, I sit in the hall and take fifteen shillings from each pupil before admitting her to the lesson."

"How many pupils?"

"An average of twenty for each class."

"Forty pupils at fifteen shillings a week. About thirty pounds. Well, that can't be enough to keep her, plus cooks and charwomen and secretaries. No income tax, I suppose?"

"The pupils pay in cash."

"Quite. Any gentlemen friends?"

I hesitated. The first male visitor to arrive after my appointment had been an elderly Italian gentleman by the name of Georgio. Without caring to appear too naive, I have to state that for some time, I accepted without reserve Madame's statement that they had been children together. It wasn't until Georgio departed after five merry weeks—which I enjoyed as much as anybody—that I discovered that the bedroom he had occupied connected with Madame's. Georgio had been followed by two or three more of Madame's childhood friends; during their visits, our standard of living rose sharply and a good deal of the furniture reappeared. I decided to say nothing of this to James Maitland; it wasn't my business—or his.

"I've had Madame in mind," he said, "ever since I realised that the Lubin plays were going to bring in money; I felt she was entitled to a share of the profits. It's pretty clear that she needs them."

"She doesn't worry about money," I said. "She doesn't worry about anything."

"You like her?"

"Very much indeed."

"You live here?"

"Yes. I wanted a living-in job."

I got up, wheeled the wagon into the dining-room, put the cups and plates on the hatch and pulled the rope to send it down to the kitchen. James Maitland followed me and watched me and listened as I addressed the cook through the speaking-tube.

"Can't be many of those things left in London," he commented.

"I don't know what we'd do without it," I said. "Madame won't go down, and the cook won't come up."

I walked into the hall, opened the letter-box and took out the afternoon post. Most of the letters were for James Maitland and most of them had been readdressed from Norway or from Paris. On two of the envelopes I recognised Neil Patterson's handwriting. I sorted the letters and handed James Maitland his; he walked back to the drawing-room and began to read them, and I left him and went out to do some shopping for Madame. I didn't see him again until we met in the drawing-room just before dinner. Madame was not yet down.

"This Neil Patterson," he began without preamble. "What do you know about him?"

"He's a well-known producer."

"I've had two letters from him and I didn't like either of them. I didn't like what I saw of him at the station, either."

"Not many people like him," I said, "but from all one hears and reads, he's a pretty successful producer. If he's going to produce your uncle's play, it's half-way to success. Neil Patterson only does what he wants to do, but what he wants to do, he does extremely well—so they tell me. I don't know anything about the theatre."

"What I wanted to know was whether you knew anything about Neil Patterson?"

"I knew him up in Scotland. His parents live near my god-mother. He didn't like me and I didn't like him and that's all I can tell you, but it isn't what you want to know. You want to know something about his theatrical background."

"No, I don't. I want to know if he's as arrogant as his letters sound. He talks about the Edinburgh Festival as though the whole thing's tied up already. He's even got a cast lined up. Have you ever heard of an actor with a name like a house— Eden Croft?"

I walked across the room, opened a cigarette-box, took a cigarette and then turned and offered one to James Maitland.

"These may not be what you like, but take one anyhow," I invited.

He took one.

"Don't you like Eden Croft either?" he asked.

"I've only seen him act in one play. He was extremely good."

"In London?"

"No. In Edinburgh."

"Touring company?"

"Yes."

Only one play—but I'd been to see it seven times. Some girls are born crazy; others go crazy at the age of twenty-four.

James Maitland held a light to my cigarette.

"You're not an easy girl to get information out of," he commented.

"Why talk to me? Why not go out and talk to managers and agents and actors and actresses?"

"There's no hurry," he said. "The Edinburgh Festival isn't until August. This is only May—and you forget that I'm more or less new to managers and agents and actors and actresses. Until last year, agents and managers used to hide behind their desks when they saw me coming. I'm glad my uncle's work is getting the recognition it deserves, and I can never explain to anybody how happy I've been for the past three years getting to know his work—but this aspect of it doesn't appeal to me."

"If you're a playwright, surely you love the theatre and everything connected with it?"

"Not necessarily. I found the rehearsals in Paris a sort of hell. I hated the whole thing. If I'd been dealing with my own original work, I would have left them to it—but I wasn't. I was dealing, or so I thought, with a trust. I felt that I had to take care of all the detail myself, and they didn't like that. That's why I don't like them. That's why I don't react too favourably when Neil Patterson or anyone else writes me letters implying that everything's all folded up and as good as in production already."

Madame came in and we said no more. We went into the dining-room and the lamb chops came up on the hatch, accompanied by peas and potatoes and the thick brown gravy in which Madame liked to float her food. The talk was of Norway.

"Why didn't you ever go back?" James asked Madame. She spread her hands wide and shrugged.

"Why? Sometimes I ask myself, but I do not know the

27

answer. I spent my youth in Norway; perhaps I do not wish to go back there and meet the ghost of this young girl, so fresh, so vital, so—this I must say, for it is true—good-looking. Perhaps I did not wish to hear my brother tell me that I had wasted my life. Perhaps I was happier in England. Certainly I am happy now to have you here with me. James, how long will you stay?"

"Can you have me until I go to Edinburgh?"

"I can have you always. I shall give you a little sitting-room downstairs for your friends. Alison and I will use the drawing-room; she does her work in the study. Whatever you want, you must ask Alison. If you want her to help you, she will do so."

The next morning, with many apologies, he asked me if I would type some letters for him and I said I would. On the following day, he left out the apologies and gave me half a dozen letters. By the end of the week he was stopping me on the stairs or in the hall, waving a bunch of papers at me and asking irritably where I had been hiding myself.

It was my job to answer all telephone calls. Several of them were from Neil Patterson. I put them through to James's sitting-room until one day Neil stopped me.

"No—don't put me on to Maitland," he said. "I'll talk to you. What's the matter with the blasted fellow? I've written to him and I've telephoned him, but all I get out of him is evasions. I've tried to make an appointment. I've invited him to lunch. I've invited him to meetings. I've invited him to dinner.

Is he going to discuss this play, or isn't he?"

"I don't know anything about the play," I said. "The only work I've done for him has been connected with his business in Norway."

"Can't you fix a time for me to come and see him—or is this a deliberate policy of avoidance?"

"I don't know."

He hung up and I went to the sitting-room and spoke to James Maitland.

"Neil Patterson thinks you're pursuing a policy of deliberate avoidance," I said.

He was at a table, working. He looked up absently.

"Eh?"

"Neil Patterson. He thinks you're avoiding him."

"So I am. I'm busy. If he rings up again, tell him I've gone back to Norway."

Neil Patterson didn't ring up again; on the following morning, he came to the house. He was dressed in slacks and a turtle-necked sweater and Madame mistook him for the electrician.

"Ah, at last!" she exclaimed, coming upon him in the hall. "Five times I have telephoned. I got a very bad shock from that switch."

I explained that he wasn't the electrician, led him to the sitting-room and shut him in with James Maitland.

"Who is he?" Madame asked.

29

"Neil Patterson."

"Should I know him?"

"He's a well-known producer. He's been asked to produce the Lubin play at the Edinburgh Festival in August."

She looked impressed.

"Is James pleased?"

"He doesn't seem interested."

"But that is nonsense!" she said angrily. "If this man is well-known, he must be listened to."

"I dare say Neil is explaining that at this moment," I said. Her face became dreamy.

"I was thinking that I would go to Innsbruck, but now I will not," she said. "I shall go to Edinburgh. We shall all go to Edinburgh. We shall drive up there. By that time, James will have a car of his own. You shall drive me; he will drive himself. We shall have picnics on the way. I shall buy a picnic hamper. A real one; a fitted one."

I left her planning picnics and went into the garden to pick flowers for the house. I came round a corner to find Neil Patterson striding down the path towards me.

"I want to talk to you," he said brusquely.

I said nothing and he followed me into the long stone corridor in which I did the flowers. It was gloomy and rather damp and not really a very good place for conversation.

"I want to tell you something," he said abruptly. "I submitted a provisional list of the cast to Maitland."

"So he told me."

"Eden's name was on it."

"Yes, so I heard."

My back was turned to him; he put a hand on my arm and pulled me round to face him.

"Look," he said, "I've got to know about this. Is it over, or isn't it over?"

"It's entirely over," I said calmly. "I told you so at the station."

"I'm sorry for what happened, Alison. I swear I am."

"So you said. But you needn't be; most of what happened was my fault."

"What I did then, I'd probably do again," he said, "but I'm sorry I did it to you. And now I've got to know whether meeting Eden again is going to make difficulties for you or not."

"Or not," I said.

"If he takes this part—it's the lead—you'll have to see a good deal of him. He'll have to come to this house. You'll have to meet him, talk to him, perhaps sit through meals with him."

"If he doesn't mind, why should I?" I inquired. "I didn't do anything."

He stared at me for some moments in silence.

"My God, you've changed!" he said slowly.

"Only back to what I was before I met Eden. I was sane enough before I met him, and once it was all over, I became

31

sane again."

"Why did you hide?" he asked.

"I didn't hide. I had to leave home. What did you expect me to do—stay for the wedding?"

"I wrote to your godmother the other day. I told her I'd seen you and I gave her your address. I told her what you were doing."

I said nothing. That had been, in a way, the worst of all. I had written once, twice, and she had not answered. She couldn't have blamed me—perhaps, I thought, she hadn't wanted to be reminded. It had been hard to stay away; it was the only home I'd ever known and I would have liked, after a time, to have gone back. I would have liked to have seen her, talked to her, stayed with her.

"Alison—"

I stepped back to see the effect of a flower arrangement.

"Well?"

"I'd take Eden's name off that list if I could; but I can't; it's too late. I offered him the part and I can't go back on the offer now. And I don't want to. I need him in the part—and he needs the part. He needs the job; he needs it badly."

I didn't have to ask why. If an actor's heading for success, you hear about him. You see his name in the papers. You read of his progress, you hear him mentioned. I knew very well what Eden's hopes had been; I knew very well that none of them had been realised.

"You can give him the job or not give him the job; it's all the same to me," I said.

Something in the way I spoke must have convinced him at last. Our eyes met, and I heard myself saying something I hadn't meant to say.

"Is he here?"

"No. He isn't in London; he's with a second-rate company touring the Midlands. Margaret's just gone up to Scotland, to her mother."

Margaret...

Margaret was with her mother, and Eden was with a second-rate company touring the Midlands. It wasn't exactly as I'd pictured them.

"It didn't work out," I heard Neil Patterson saying. "Nothing worked out. But I don't suppose you're interested."

"Not very," I said.

I turned to take some flowers out of the water, and once again—but more gently—Neil turned me round to face him.

"Let's be friends, Alison. Please."

It was the first time I had ever seen, ever heard anything in him that could explain why so many people could overlook his broodingly insolent look, his arrogant manner. The dark eyes fixed on me were still deep and unreadable, but his expression was no longer aloof, his voice no longer abrupt. I could see some reason, at last, for his friends' patience and loyalty.

"Please," he said again. "I've got to spend a lot of time

with Maitland, and this house is the best meeting-place we've got. If you face the truth, you'll have to acknowledge that what I did in enmity proved to be, for you, an act of salvation. That doesn't wipe out the past, but it does mean that we can try to come to terms now. All I'm suggesting is a fresh start. You're working here, I'm working here; we meet frequently—we have to. So let's meet on new ground and get on to adult terms. Let's meet, let's talk, let's behave in a natural, friendly way. It can be done, and it's a good thing to do. Do you agree?"

"We never liked one another," I reminded him.

"How do you know we didn't? I was a bloody-minded little boy and you were a poor little devil of an orphan who'd had the luck to fall into good hands but who was probably going through a hell of a time trying to get readjusted. Will you start again now, or won't you?"

"When I saw you at the station," I said slowly, "I was afraid—but not for long. I needn't have been afraid. It was all over. I realised then that I was really free; free of you all. I'd like to stay that way."

"Margaret's up in Scotland; I'll see that Eden keeps out of your way. That leaves myself. You and I will have to meet in the future whether you like it or not. When the Festival's over, I'm going home for a time. When your godmother gets in touch with you again, you'll be going home too. As close neighbours, it'll be impossible to go on avoiding one another. Will you agree at least to a truce?"

He put out a hand, palm uppermost, as we had done as

children when choosing sides for games.

"Friend or foe?" he asked, as we had asked long ago.

I hesitated, but not for long. What he had said was true, and it was also sensible. We were bound to meet; we could meet on a new basis. I had nothing to lose, nothing to fear. I laid my palm for an instant on his.

"Let's just call it a truce" I said.

Chapter Two

James Maitland wasn't long in making his aunt's house his own. He was not a tidy man; his bedroom each morning presented such a spectacle of scattered shirts, slacks and socks, that soon the daily women refused to do more than the basic cleaning, and left the tidying to me. His sitting-room was a litter of papers, but he allowed nobody to tidy these or even to touch them. He got up early, went downstairs and had his breakfast in the kitchen and was usually out of the house before ten. He lunched with Madame and myself and spent the afternoon doing some form of exercise, coming back to a late tea. Nobody knew very much about his preoccupations; he didn't say and Madame didn't ask. But about a week after Neil Patterson had paid his visit to the house, he came again by invitation and the two men spent a long morning together. After this, Neil came almost every day.

Working conditions in the house were of course ideal. If James Maitland had not possessed the trait to an even more marked degree, he must have noticed and been grateful to Madame for her total lack of curiosity in the affairs of others. She minded her own business because her own business interested her far more than other people's business.

This self-absorption had been my chief source of comfort during my early months with her. She wasn't particularly selfish; it was simply that running her own life took up all her time, leaving none over for peering into other people's windows. When something unusual caught or was brought to her attention, she made the appropriate comments, acted if action was necessary—and retreated once more within the circle of her own world. It was a small world, but it was a busy enough one. The classes absorbed a certain amount of her time; for the rest, there were quarrels with the cook, arguments with the daily women over the elaborate work schedules she had drawn up and which they consistently ignored; encounters with tradespeople who grew restive over bills; endless, exhausting sessions with dressmakers and milliners who refused, not without reason, to execute her original but extraordinary designs. There were visits to galleries to see exhibitions of pictures or furniture; she also attended every mannequin parade to which she could gain admission. Most of her occupations were trivial, but they filled her day and her mind and rendered her oblivious to the concerns of others.

I observed the same detachment in James Maitland; he was busy, and evinced no interest in Madame or myself or in anybody else. He gave me an increasing number of letters to type, but he spent less and less time in the house and soon began to take lunch and dinner elsewhere. He and Madame went their own way; I went mine. I arranged interviews for new pupils, I saw that the house was kept clean, I did the shopping and drove Madame about in her car.

Another similarity between aunt and nephew, I learned, was their complete unconcern with regard to their appearance. Londoners, accustomed to strange sights, rarely gave a second glance at Madame's odd outfits, but James's ill-fitting suits came in for more attention. The ten-year-old twin terrors in one of the flats next door had taken to leaning over their balcony as he passed, yelling *'French sailor trousers! Toulon and Toulouse!'*

It was too much to hope that Madame would notice anything extraordinary about her nephew's appearance, but I felt that since he was so much in the public eye, something ought to be done about it; somebody should at least see that he had his hair cut; it was creeping down into his collar.

I decided at last to make use of Madame's passion for planning, and placed on her breakfast tray cards from a local hairdresser and tailor.

"They're new to the district, and they'd like you to recommend them," I told her. "Perhaps Mr. Maitland could make use of them."

"You must call him James, Alison; he has asked you to, many times."

"Perhaps James could make use of them."

It was only a lead, but she followed it and for the first time scrutinised her nephew. Disliking what she saw, she kept her attention on him long enough to ensure that his jackets were made more shapely and his trousers more safe. His hair was cut. His tattered socks and shabby shirts were renewed. Before she lost interest, she had smartened him up considerably. He didn't look handsome, but he looked neat—which was as well, because Neil Patterson had a wide and influential circle of friends and was beginning to draw him into it. He met the Press. He met an interested section of the public and he met the cast—and after that, I knew it couldn't be long before Eden Croft came to Cranston Avenue.

The Press began to be troublesome. I had no experience of dealing with reporters, by telephone or in person, but as James Maitland refused to see or talk to them, I became adept in a sort of non-committal politeness. Yes, Mr. Maitland was working on *Fairground.* Yes, Mr. Patterson would produce. No, the full cast had not as yet been agreed upon. Yes, the first performance would be at the Edinburgh Festival.

I had had, to my joy, a letter from my godmother. It was brief, and it contained no reference whatsoever to the past; it said simply that she had heard good news of me and would like to see me. Was there any chance of my coming up during the summer?

I thought that there was a very good chance, for it was becoming clear that when *Fairground* went to Edinburgh, Madame would go too. If Madame went, I would have to go with her. I wrote to my godmother to this effect; like her, I made no reference to the past.

When James came into the study one morning, to bring some work that he wanted typed, he paused to make an additional request.

"There's going to be a sort of meeting here tomorrow morning; some fellows will be along at about eleven. Could you arrange beer or coffee or both?"

I said that I could.

"This fellow Croft is coming. Patterson says you know him quite well. Why didn't you tell me that when I mentioned him before?"

"You asked me if he could act and I told you that he could act extremely well. I thought you were interested in him professionally, not personally."

"All I'm worried about is whether Patterson's interested in him personally and not professionally. I don't mind taking his word when he tells me that Croft is one of the best actors in the country; that's something I can check for myself. But why hasn't more been heard of him? Why has this best-actor-in-the-country been doing what he's been doing? Why didn't the Press give him a write-up when the cast list was published? My own idea is that Patterson's trying to do him a good turn, and if a cold fish of a fellow like Patterson does anybody a good turn, I've got a feeling there must be something fishy behind it."

"They've been close friends for years. They went through school together, and never lost touch."

"Then why has he waited until now to give him a good part? He's been producing plays successfully for eight years or more. Why hasn't Croft been given the lead in those?—How long have you known Croft?"

"I met him about two years ago. He married my godmother's daughter."

"Actress?"

"No."

He stared moodily at me.

"I don't suppose you care whether this play's a hit or a miss," he said. "All the same, if you know anything about Croft that's likely to prejudice its success, I'd like to hear it."

"I can't tell you anything about him that Neil doesn't know. He's ambitious, and I understand that this play's giving him a good chance of going to the top. If that's the case, you don't have to worry about him."

"I'll worry all the same," James said as he went out.

Eden Croft came to the meeting. I saw his car outside and heard him talking to Neil Patterson as they crossed the hall on their way to the study. Madame was out. At about midday, I sent the daily woman in with a wagon on which I'd put beer and coffee. Ten minutes later, I heard James Maitland shouting my name.

"Alison! Could you come in here and take some notes?" I went in. James, looking preoccupied, waved a hand towards the seven men present and mumbled some names. "Oh, you

41

know Croft, don't you?" he said.

"Yes." I smiled across the room. "Hallo, Eden." My voice sounded quiet, natural and friendly. "How's Margaret?"

He said that Margaret was well and that she was up in Scotland. Would she be coming to London? No; she was to stay in Edinburgh until he joined her. Well, I would look forward to seeing her up there.

I sat down and took the notes James Maitland wanted to give me. Whenever I raised my eyes, I saw that Eden was watching me and that Neil Patterson was watching Eden, but all I felt was a kind of light-headed happiness. I'd met him, I'd spoken to him. If his eyes were as clear as Neil's, he must have seen that whatever I had once felt, I wasn't feeling it now.

When I went out of the room, I took with me an absolutely clear picture of him. I took it into the study and, sitting at my desk, set the picture up mentally in front of me. I wanted to examine it. I wanted to find out, if I could, what power, what magnetism it held to have had so devastating an effect on me.

It couldn't, I decided after a long scrutiny, have been only his face. It was undeniably handsome, but there was no line on it of strength or of purpose. There wasn't even, I realised with an odd sense of mingled shame and pity, any sign of ordinary good sense. For the first time, I saw him through my godmother's eyes and realised how helpless, how desperate she must have felt.

His voice... That, at any rate, was by any standards beautiful. I had arrived at the theatre, the first time, very late; the first act was more than half over. He had been on the stage alone, reading aloud a letter he held in his hands. It was a love letter, and he read it like a man who returned, fully and passionately, the love that it expressed. I was with some friends in the back of the stalls, a long way from the stage. ...

It seemed impossible that I could sit here, feeling nothing at all, and still have the power to re-create those first moments. I could remember, now, exactly what I felt then—but now it was in my head and no longer in my heart.

It's said that you never realise how ill you've been until you've fully recovered. This must be particularly true of passion, for at that moment I could estimate fully what I'd been through. With Eden Croft's handsome, empty face clearly before me, I could also estimate fully what I had escaped. Seeing him clearly at last, and knowing Margaret as I did, I could guess why things hadn't worked out.

After that morning, Eden came frequently to the house and I was interested, but not surprised, to see Madame succumbing to his charm. It was the more potent, I saw at last, because he made so little use of it. So little conscious use. He made no effort to charm Madame, but before long, she was issuing invitations to him to lunch and to dine, and insisting upon James being present at at least a few meals during the week.

Between meals, she began to give interviews to the Press; she was photographed and appeared in the papers as Madame Lubin, the sister of the famous Norwegian playwright; the class numbers rose from twenty to thirty and more and more letters appeared on her breakfast tray.

We saw very little of James in between meals, but I was able to trace his movements and in fact follow in his tracks, for he always took his umbrella out with him and seldom brought it back. I was sent on most mornings-after to retrieve it from restaurants, from theatres, sometimes from private houses or flats. In anybody else, I would have begun to suspect that this refusal to appear on the sunniest of days without a large black umbrella denoted a desire to create an interesting or amusing image in the public mind—but James Maitland, submitting to publicity as an inevitable appendage to success, never went out of his way to seek it.

When I returned one morning from yet another journey to retrieve his umbrella, I found him waiting impatiently for me in the study.

"Where've you been all this time?" he demanded.

"Umbrella-chasing. Why don't you hang it on the back of your collar?"

He laid some papers on my desk, drove his hands deep into the pockets of his trousers and stood frowning down at me.

"What made me think of taking up play-writing as a profession?" he asked gloomily.

"You tell me," I invited. "But not this minute; I've got a lot to do."

"You've always got a lot to do. What the hell it all is, I've never been able to discover. What does Madame want with a secretary in the first place?"

"Secretary-companion."

"Companion, perhaps—but secretary? Why a secretary?"

"You put your finger on it when you said in the first place. She engaged her first secretary when she settled in England. In those days, she used to form societies."

"Religious?"

"No." I pointed to a carved wooden chest standing in a corner of the room. "The evidence is all in there, neatly filed by my predecessors. *The-Norway-in-London-Society. The-Norwegian-Ladies-London-Literary-Society.* And so on. Later, I think, money became more of a problem, and she began to give lessons in Norwegian. But there didn't seem any great rush to learn Norwegian, and so she began her present classes. By that time, the secretary had become a habit and I don't think you'll ever break her of it." I paused. "She can act rather rashly sometimes. If she hadn't someone to straighten things out for her, she'd get involved in a lot of schemes that would lead nowhere."

"Or lead to trouble. I see. Well, if you can sort out her problems, maybe you'd have a shot at clearing up mine. Did you or did you not tell me that Croft and Patterson had been buddies from boyhood?"

"I said they were—"

"—close friends for years, went through school together, never lost touch. Then why, to put it mildly, do they hate one another's guts?"

"They don't."

"Oh, but they do."

"A man doesn't offer an important leading part to—"

"Patterson made the offer by wire. He and Croft hadn't met, he told me, for about eighteen months. They met again here in London, and the first time I saw them together, I admit that they had some resemblance to that picture you painted. But not any more. Something's broken up that long, sweet friendship. It wouldn't be you, by any chance?"

"It's a good thing you weren't a doctor; you're not too good on diagnosis."

"All right; it isn't you; so what is it? Everybody can feel the tension. I suggested to Patterson that Croft might feel better if his wife was closer at hand—but that appeared to be another wrong diagnosis."

"This play means a lot to them both; couldn't it be nerves?"

"Could be. Is that the only solution you have to offer?"

"I'm a secretary-companion—and chauffeur on the side. Within those limits, I'd be glad to help you. Please shut the door as you go out."

He banged it so hard that the house shook. But at least he was outside and I could get on with my work.

He surprised me at dinner a week later by telling me without preamble that Margaret was in London.

"Your cousin's here," he said. "Have you seen her?"

"My cousin?" I repeated, bewildered.

"Isn't Croft married to your cousin?"

"No. We're no relation."

"Where did I get the idea that you were?"

"She's my godmother's daughter. My parents died when I was four or five and my godmother brought me up—but we're not related. Is she in London?"

"She's been in London for the past five days. I'd think that my diagnosis wasn't so far wrong if it weren't for the fact that her husband (*a*) didn't send for her and (*b*) has been, if possible, even more impossible since her arrival. Why hasn't she let you know she was here?"

"I suppose she's busy," I said.

Five days. Margaret had been in London for five days. My godmother's letter had told me that she was at home; there had been no mention of her coming to join Eden. She had sent her love to me—no letter, but her love. And she had been in London for five days without letting me know, without sending any message ...

I heard Madame speaking indignantly.

"She is very impolite, this woman. She drives her husband to my house, and she sits outside and waits for him without entering. This is one thing—but yesterday, as I was in the street speaking with somebody, the car came and Mr. Croft said 'This is my wife.' 'Ah, please to come in,' I said—and what does she do? She looks at me without any expression at all, without any smile, and says 'I'm sorry, I am busy'—and drives away. You know something, James? When I see all these theatre people, I do not think much of them. They are not people I would like to know better."

"Margaret isn't in the theatre," I said.

Madame looked surprised.

"No? She is very good-looking. She has the air of an actress. But all the same, I find her rather insolent."

She wasn't the first to use that adjective when speaking of Margaret. I opened my mouth to explain that most of Margaret's manner was merely a cover for shyness, but closed it again, as Madame's interest, seldom deep, had evaporated, and she was asking James about the cast.

"Six men, one woman" he said. "But this time, it isn't the woman who's making trouble."

I had ceased to listen to the conversation; I was weighing the reasons for Margaret's avoidance of me. I wondered if she had decided that no good could come of a reunion. She had come to join Eden, but there was no need for her to run across me unless she wanted to. About Eden's feelings on the matter I was even less sure. Though he had seen me frequently on his visits to the house, he had, since our first encounter, done no more than pass the time of day. I couldn't explain to myself why I imagined that when we came upon one another in the hall or on the stairs, he seemed to be on the verge of pausing to speak to me. On two occasions, I had come out of the study and seen him standing in the hall and had been left with the impression that he had been about to enter the room—but on each occasion he had, to my relief, turned and walked away without a word.

Now Margaret was here, and, like Eden, was keeping out of my way.

The days went by and she neither wrote nor phoned. She came to the house, but only to leave Eden and drive away again. It wasn't until the last week of June that we met. I had been on an errand for James Maitland and got back to the house just as Margaret was leaving it. We came face to face.

She was in her own small, open sports car. She was wearing a black suit and a small emerald green hat that hid all her hair and showed her face in all its pure beauty. She stared at me expressionlessly for a few moments through the windscreen and then switched off the engine. I walked up to the car and halted beside it.

"Hallo, Margaret. It's been a long time," I said. "Coming in?"

"No. I almost did once, but I caught sight of that frightful fat woman and fled." She leaned over and opened the car door. "Get in," she invited.

I got in and with difficulty got James Maitland's umbrella in too.

"Why in the world are you walking round with a man's umbrella?" she inquired in amazement.

"It belongs to James Maitland. He's always leaving it around. He leaves it in buses and restaurants and shops and I have to retrieve it. He treasures it."

"Why?"

"It was presented to him by the people of Transel."

"They must have subscribed generously," she said dryly.

"There's a lot of silver on the handle."

We stared at the handle together. We stared at it for quite a long time, seemingly absorbed. It was almost midday and the sun was warm. From the upper windows of the house came the voice of the daily woman raised in song.

"Is that the woman they call Madame?" Margaret inquired.

"No."

"How can you work for her? She looks like something that Wagner saw in a nightmare."

"The work's easy and she doesn't interfere."

She sat silent for some moments.

"Have you read the play?" she asked.

"Yes."

"What did you make of it?"

I hesitated. I hadn't been able to make head or tail. I was pretty sure Madame hadn't understood it either, but she had claimed to have been unable to read for the tears that blinded her, to have been unable to put down the play until she had finished it and to have been unable to sleep when she did at last put it down. I was willing to concede that the Norwegian background made more sense to her than it did to me.

"I'm not much good at reading plays," I said. "I'll have to wait until I see it performed."

"If it ever gets performed," she said.

I turned to stare at her.

"Who'll stop it?" I inquired.

"Several things. Eden for one. He loathes James Maitland and James Maitland knows it and doesn't mind. He may know something about playwrights, but he knows nothing at all about actors; he's under the impression that all they have to do is act. Neil's been trying to make him see that before they act, they have to be conditioned; they have to be consulted and cosseted and humoured, handled with care and allowed to have their own way in everything that doesn't matter. This part's made for Eden and Eden's made for the part, but when it comes to interpretation, all three of them pull different ways—Neil, Eden and this Maitland. Neil knows how to cope with Eden, and he also knows all there is to know about most playwrights he's dealt with—but Maitland hasn't once given way on any single point, and has made it clear that he despises and dislikes both Eden and Neil."

I heard a voice speaking in mild defence of James Maitland and to my surprise realised that it was my own.

"He's got this sacred-trust attitude to his uncle's work. He regards himself as—"

"All he's done is translate some of the works and bring them to the notice of a wider public. Had you ever heard of Lubin before the beginning of this year?"

I had to admit that I hadn't.

"Of course not. Nobody had—nobody at the popular level, that is. Did you know that Neil had gone over to Paris?"

"No."

"Well, he has. He's gone over to talk to the man who put on the Lubin play over there and the reason I'm sitting in this car now is because Eden seized the opportunity of coming to talk to James Maitland alone. See what I mean? A nice, co-operative trio."

I said nothing, being busy with the reflection that after all that had happened between us, Margaret and I were this morning sitting in a busy London street engaged in conversation about nothing more controversial than a Norwegian playwright. It wasn't, I decided, so very odd. We couldn't talk about the past, we didn't know much about the future; the sanest, the safest thing to do was to talk about the present. But suddenly she moved without warning into last year's shadows.

"You should have written to my mother when you left home," she said. "If you'd seen her when she got Neil's letter, and then yours. . ."

"I wrote twice. I told Neil so when I met him at the station."

"Why would letters go astray if you posted them? She would have got them."

"I did post them, and she didn't get them."

"She thought you ... that you'd ..."

There was silence. I knew very well what she must have thought.

"You're going home, aren't you?" she said after a time. "You promised my mother you would."

"Madame is going up to the Festival and I'll have to go with her. She'll be playing the lead-off stage. She can come back to London with James Maitland and I'll go home."

Home...

"Are you happy?" she asked.

"Yes."

I didn't put the question to her. I didn't have to. Nobody could look at her dark, desperate eyes and ask if she was happy. I wouldn't have had to look into her eyes; knowing her as I had done all my life, I could have read the truth in the set of her head, in her restless hands, in her dry, brittle sentences. It wouldn't do to ask her if she was happy.

I opened the car door suddenly and got out.

"We ought to talk sometimes," she said. "I mean talk."

I didn't reply. We looked at one another for a moment and then I turned and ran up the stairs and opened the door of the house, and, without a backward glance, went inside and closed it behind me.

Chapter Three

When Neil returned from Paris, he brought with him the girl who was to play the lead opposite Eden. She was a Swedish actress named Christina Hedberg; previously unknown, she had achieved fame by her performance in the Lubin play in Paris. She had naturally blonde hair, ice-blue eyes and a creamy skin; Neil brought her to the house and her arrival caused James Maitland to lose something of his detachment. Watching their reunion, I interpreted it to mean that they were about to pick up where they'd left off.

There was from that moment an even further reduction in the number of lunches and dinners he ate at home. Madame, whom Christina had failed to impress, voiced her resentment to me over her breakfast tray.

"If I had known how it would be," she said "I would never have asked him to come here. When I asked him to come, did I expect that he would use me simply as bed and breakfast? You see yourself that he does this. He fills my house with men who do not speak to me, who scarcely give me the courtesy of saying Good morning or Good evening or Hallo or Good-bye—except Mr. Croft, who is different from the rest. They consider me only as an old worn-out aunt earning money by giving some classes. I have explained who I am. It has been in all the papers." She buttered a slice of toast with such angry energy that it broke into pieces. "I am nearer, much nearer to Olav than James. Olav was my brother; I was his favourite sister. We played together; we grew up together. When he began to write, to whom did he read his work? To me. When he was honoured at last with the Nobel prize for literature, to whom did he first tell the news? To myself. Did he expect that when his work was performed for the first time in England that—oh, very well, very well; in Scotland, if you wish—did he expect that I would be ignored and pushed aside, made nothing of? If a man is famous, do they not wish to know something of his beginnings? Who can tell them? Only I. But who asks me? Nobody."

I looked at her red, angry countenance.

"Couldn't you," I suggested, "write some of it down?" She stared at me uncomprehendingly.

"Write it down? You mean write a book about Lubin? How can I write a book? I don't know how to write a book."

"I didn't mean a book. I meant one or two articles about him. I could help you. I could take them down as you dictate them, and type them out. You could perhaps sell them to a newspaper or a magazine."

She sat silently speculating on the project, and then spoke with determination.

"I shall do this. I shall begin today," she said. "You should have told me this before, that I could write down what I know of him. I shall say it, and you shall put it down."

James made one of his rare appearances at dinner, and she told him what she planned to do.

"Go ahead," he said amiably but rather absently. "But don't be too long in bringing it out. The public interest comes—and goes."

"And a great man—is he to be of passing and not of lasting interest?" demanded Madame angrily.

She had never before addressed him in anything but a friendly tone. I saw him look at her in surprise.

"The play's the thing, surely?" he pointed out mildly.

"The play is not the only thing. The man is also something. I am of course pleased, I am grateful, that you have made more people in the world aware of your uncle, but I am not pleased that you think only of his work and not of him. He suffered—did you know that? He was lonely and sad."

"Sometimes," James said.

"He loved a girl called Katrina and she died and that was when he began first to write. When you were there in Transel, did you visit her grave and read the words he wrote for her gravestone?"

"Never."

"No, you did none of this. And since you came here to this house, nobody has been interested to ask me anything, but I am going to write down all these things, because they should be known. I thought when you came here that you and I would talk about him, but you do not talk about him. You do not talk of anything. In fact you do not talk, at least not to me. But I am not unhappy about this. Today, for the first time, I feel that Olav Lubin is in this house. He is here and I shall speak for him. Alison shall write it down, and perhaps when it is all written down you will be interested to read it, if you can spare time from running after actresses."

She pushed her chair back and rose; James opened the door for her. He closed it behind her and we heard her going upstairs to her room. Coming back to the table, he sat down and looked across at me with raised eyebrows.

"Since when?" he inquired.

"It's been simmering," I explained. "But I think it's a good idea; don't you?"

"It might be interesting—if she can do it?"

"Why shouldn't she be able to do it?"

"He and she weren't together much when they were young. One-eighth will be fact and the rest not very good fiction."

"Did you know about Katrina, who loved him, and the words on her tombstone?"

"Of course I knew. I spent three years over in Norway, getting to know. My uncle was the nation's prize hoarder; he never threw anything away in his life, and that includes letters. Madame has forgotten that he left me all his papers, and that didn't mean only his work. It meant more or less everything he'd ever written down. Going through the accumulation—it took me most of the first year—I learnt about Katrina, and also about Marianne and Inga and Anna and some others."

"Did he write lines for all their tombstones?"

"Not as far as I know—but the whole of the big scene in *Fairground* is lifted straight from an exchange of letters between him and a woman called Elisa. My uncle was twenty three at the time, and she was forty-three. They were beautiful letters and it's a beautiful scene."

"What happened to Elisa?"

"She married a merchant in Hanover and died full of riches. But that, and many other things, Madame doesn't know."

"She probably knows a little more about his childhood than you do."

"Haven't you forgotten that I've just spent three years among people who grew up with him? I met his schoolmates and his schoolmasters and talked to frail old ladies who remembered going tobogganing with him. But all that interested me was his work. Madame didn't seem to like Christina Hedberg. What do you think of her?"

"Sensational. She must be the first Swedish actress who's ever appeared in Scotland in the English translation of a Norwegian playwright's second play after she'd appeared in Paris in a French translation of his first play."

Treating this with the contempt it merited, he pushed his coffee-cup towards me and I refilled it.

"You're not exactly the person to help Madame with her reminiscences," he commented.

"Why not?"

"Because you're an ingrowing person and not given to delving into the past. For example, you've been with Madame for well over a year and she knows hardly anything about you."

"Madame, like yourself," I said, "has very little curiosity about other people."

"And if she'd had any curiosity, and tried to satisfy it, she'd probably have got as far as I did when I asked you about Patterson and Croft. Incidentally, wasn't that Croft's wife you were talking to outside the house the other morning?"

"Yes."

"You might ask her what there is about us all that she dislikes so much. She sits out there in that car like a chauffeur. Chauffeuse. Why did she change her mind and leave Scotland? Croft's been giving us a lot more trouble since she joined him. He was just settling down, becoming a team member."

The idea of Eden Croft becoming a team member was so new that I was driven to an unwary comment.

"It sounds unlikely," I said, and found his eyes resting speculatively on mine.

"You don't like him, do you? And you don't like Patterson—and you and Croft's wife were brought up together, so she sits outside and avoids running into you. What did you all quarrel about?"

59

"I thought playwrights were supposed to be observant," I said. "I thought they stood back and viewed life with keen eyes that missed nothing—detached reporters. You're detached enough, but I can't say much for your eyesight."

"What makes you say I'm detached?"

I held up one of the fingers of my right hand; round it was wound an adhesive bandage.

"This, for one thing. For one out of a hundred small things. You and Madame both require my services as a typist, but it hasn't occurred to either of you today to ask how I hurt my finger, or whether typing will be difficult. Relax; I can still type."

"How did you hurt your finger, dear Miss Sinclair?—Is that the right shade of anxious interest?"

"It doesn't have to be anxious; it doesn't even have to be interest; I'm only pointing out that you don't seem to notice much about people, and I would have said that that was your job."

"I wasn't very good at my job. Remember that the success in Paris wasn't mine; it was my uncle's. If you want a more perfect specimen to pin that detached label on to, it's yourself. You remind me of a frozen pond, and a frozen pond doesn't give an observer much to work on. All one can do is stand on the edge and watch people like Patterson and Croft skating dangerously over the thin ice. Sometimes I'd like to tell them that they might fall in and find it extremely cold, but I don't do that because it's their affair and I believe that people of their age ought to be able to manage their own affairs. This sharing-one's-troubles idea is nice on paper, but it usually means taking the burden off your own shoulders and strapping it on to the most husky bystander in sight. I'm sorry I don't appear to good advantage as an observer or if I display a distressing lack of sympathy for your injuries—but on the other hand, if this play runs into trouble, you won't have me coming whining round your skirts."

He got up and without ceremony strode out of the room, leaving the door open. He went upstairs and I was left alone.

Nobody likes to be called a frozen pond. I got up and walked to one of the mirrors and took a long, sober look at myself. Age twenty-six, average height, good skin, the fair-to-red hair many Scottish girls have, small features, nice figure and neat clothes. A general air of good sense. You could see hundreds of me in the streets of Edinburgh, tweed-clad, self-possessed, going about their business. There didn't seem any frozen pond anywhere. I comforted myself by remembering that a man who could make mistakes about Neil Patterson and Eden Croft might also trip up over a character sketch of me.

I cleared the table, sent the hatch downstairs and went up to bed. Lying in the dark, I considered seriously the possibility—or even the advisability—of giving up the job. I knew that this year and a half had been a period of convalescence. The patient had been given something not too difficult to do, something not too stimulating in which to take an interest.

There had been change of scene, a quiet life, mild amusement. There had been no reference whatsoever to the painful past, no probing, no veiled curiosity, no cautious trying of locked doors. I had found the job almost by chance; I knew it now for the luckiest chance of my life. In the unlikely shelter of Madame and her house, I had come back to health and humour and happiness. And now, I realised, it was time to go on to something else, something that called for more effort, that demanded more of me mentally than this day-to-day attention to Madame's narrow needs.

Before I slept, my mind was made up. I would go up to Edinburgh—back, as I had told Margaret, to my godmother's house. When I left it again, it would not be to return to Madame or even to return to London. I had come to London to lose myself among its millions; now I wanted to be back in Scotland, meeting and mingling with all my old friends, or making new ones. I wouldn't tell Madame yet—in her own way, she liked me and would be reluctant to make a change.

I came down to breakfast earlier than usual, to find James Maitland pulling up the hatch and taking from it a loaded tray.

"Good morning. I thought you always had breakfast in the kitchen," I said in surprise.

"That was only to get the cook into training. If I'd ordered all this on the first morning, she'd have left on the spot."

"I'm sure she would," I agreed, surveying porridge, cream, bacon and eggs and tomatoes, toast, butter, honey and hot coffee.

"I went down at first and talked Norwegian and drank coffee with her. Later, I asked for toast. Then porridge. Then eggs. She enjoyed our little chats together, but she began to find that they took up too much of her morning; she decided that it would be better to send the things up to the dining-room and ... I beg your pardon—how is your finger? I see you've hurt it."

I was at the speaking-tube, ordering my coffee. Waiting beside the hatch, I watched him trying to funnel sips of coffee through a mouthful of porridge.

"You notice," he said, through another mouthful, "that I take salt with my porridge."

"Salt *to* your porridge."

"I'll make a note of that. I might have a scene just like this one in my next play."

"Try to induce your male character not to talk with his mouth full."

My coffee came up, with milk in a jug no bigger than a thimble. I saw James push the cream jug cautiously behind his coffee-pot.

"I don't take cream," I told him.

"You should. My recent resolve to notice all that goes on round me makes me aware that you're too thin, as Madame herself said. But my cream is, after all, my cream. They tell me that Scotland's like Norway. Is that true?"

"I've never been to Norway."

"I think it's the most beautiful country in the world."

"You've never been to Scotland."

He took a piece of toast and put it on his plate and covered it carefully, lovingly, with one of his fried eggs. He cut it into squares and topped each square with a crisp sliver of bacon. The smell crept across the table and mingled with the smell of my coffee and made me long suddenly for a breakfast just like the one on the tray. If I had known him better, or liked him more, I would have asked for a bite; as it was, I thought that if I drank my coffee slowly, he might go away and leave a slice of toast. He went away, but he left nothing. Nothing but the crockery. He came back to throw me a careless request.

"If Madame can spare you," he said, "and if the doctor allows you to use your damaged finger, I'd be glad if you'd type some letters for me. Oh, I'm sorry. I omitted to ask how you happened to injure yourself."

"I was walking along the Embankment when I was accosted by a large, bearded man. He was carrying a knife. When I resisted his..."

He closed the door and I went up to Madame's room and found her finishing her breakfast.

"Good morning, Alison—I have been waiting for you," she said. "See—I have already been making some notes about my brother. Just little things, as they come into my mind."

She groped for the notes and I helped her. They were on the backs of envelopes and on the unwritten-on ends of the letters she had received that morning; some were under the tray, one was pushed under her pillow, two had fallen between the bed and the wall.

"If you sit down, I will dictate" she said when I had crawled out from under the bed.

I sat down and opened my notebook.

"First, I will say about his childhood," she began. "What shall we call this ? Early days."

Early days. I wrote.

"Here is what I have put... No, that is not the sheet. Here it is. Early days. Will you underline that?"

I did so.

"*Early days*. My brother Olav was a delicate child. He—" Madame paused. "They said he was delicate, but I promise you that I myself was less strong than he. But I was a girl and he was the boy that my parents had always preferred, and so my complaints went for nothing. Often when I was sitting at my desk at school, I suffered from pains, for I had a weak stomach—or from headaches, because in those days I needed glasses. But nobody interested themselves in my needs. When we grew older, it was the same—all the care, all the attention for him and for my sister, none for myself. The more I think of those days, the more I wonder that after so much neglect I should still retain my happy nature, my gaiety. When I used to go to parties, everybody asked who was the young girl who was so full of life and sparkle."

Outgrew weak stomach, I noted.

"My brother was not kind. Always he teased me. When I had a new dress, or did my hair a new way, he never complimented me. It was always a remark to spoil my pleasure in myself. When I was with young men who admired, who loved, who courted me, I used to dread to meet my brother for fear of how he would spoil everything. I used to see him a long, long way away and took care to avoid him."

Outgrew need for glasses, I wrote.

I thought of steering her back to the subject, but decided it would scarcely be worth while; what did emerge of her brother's boyhood showed that, as James had said, he had spent very little time at home. Perhaps he had really been the favourite child, for his parents, incessant travellers, had always taken him with them and left his sisters behind. If anybody was to fill in those early years of his, it would have to be a mobile reporter.

I went downstairs wondering how I was to deal with my notes, and met Neil Patterson walking into the study.

"Too busy to talk?" he asked.

"Yes."

"Then just listen."

I looked at his dark, unreadable face and thought that time was turning him more and more into a satyr. His eyes seemed narrower and deeper and darker, his mouth more sardonic. All he needed, I thought, was horns and a tail.

"Listen to what?" I asked.

"We're going to have trouble with Eden."

"That's your worry. Why did you let him come here? Why didn't you keep him away?"

"It was all over. You said so yourself."

"So it is. But he can't enjoy having me around."

"What was I to do? Ask Maitland to come out of this house every time we needed to see him? You were the one I worried about. I didn't anticipate trouble from Eden. Not over you. Aren't we all grown up, for God's sake?" He came up and leaned against the desk at which I was sitting and stared down at me, speaking slowly and clearly. "Look, Alison; I've said this before, but it's worth saying again. This is Eden's chance. This is his big, his only, certainly his last chance. I'm offering it to him, I'm risking my own future, because this is my big chance too. This is something I've waited for for a long, long time—a great play from a great man. I've had success, but not success at this level. What I'm after now is a chance to show that I can do even better with a Lubin work than they did in Paris."

"What makes you think Eden's going to be unco-operative?"

"Instinct, and my knowledge of him. He was beginning to behave well—outwardly. He was beginning to listen—to co-operate. He doesn't like Maidand, but he'd got his dislike under cover. Then Margaret appeared and now something's got to be done."

"Why don't you do it?"

"I can't, without your help."

I laughed. It wasn't one of those hollow, sarcastic sounds—it was a laugh of pure amusement. Listening to it, Neil's face went dark with rage.

"If you laugh again," he said quietly and evenly, "I shall hit you."

"You would, too," I said. "One thing I'll never understand to my dying day is how someone like you ever happened to ordinary decent parents like yours. If I ever wrote a story about changelings, I'd use you."

"In the meantime, listen to what I'm saying. Talk to Margaret. Make her see that Eden could settle down to work with one of you around, but not both of you. She hadn't planned to come to London; in fact, she'd stated clearly that she was going to stay in Scotland until Eden joined her there. 1 don't know what brought her down, but you've got to make her go away. You can't be expected to get out of the way; you've got a job here. She hasn't."

"She's got a husband here."

"She's left him before; she can leave him again. If she doesn't, he'll get troublesome and if he gets troublesome I'll have to throw him out. If I throw him out, I'll lose my chance and he'll lose his. I can't handle Eden in this mood and Maitland too."

I looked up at him.

"Do you really imagine," I asked "that anything I could say to Margaret would have the slightest effect? I don't want to bring out any old cliches about water under the bridge, but wouldn't you say that the bridge had been washed away? How can I, of all people, tell her that her husband will work better if she goes away? And why should you imagine that your chances, or Eden's chances interest me? Nobody but you could make a suggestion of that kind."

"Will you talk to her?"

"No, I won't."

"Supposing Maitland asked you to. Would you do it then?"

"No, I wouldn't."

"It's his play. He wants the best. Aren't you interested in him either?"

"Not in the least. You'll have trouble with Eden even if you get rid of Margaret and get rid of me too. You'll have trouble with Eden because no producer ever got anything out of him but trouble. I would have said," I ended recklessly, "that you'd done enough for Eden."

His expression frightened me, but I put a sheet of paper into the typewriter and hoped that I looked like a woman intent on her work.

"What about that truce?" I heard him ask.

"Well, what about it?"

69

"We're quarrelling again, and that won't get either of us anywhere."

"If somebody has to talk to Margaret, why don't you do it? And while you're at it, ask her why she's still avoiding me. She said we ought to have a talk, and that's what I think, too. But not a talk about Eden."

"I told Eden to keep away from you. He didn't like it. Did he get hold of you while I was away in Paris?"

"No, he didn't."

"He'd like to. Any other man would be going out of his way to keep out of your way—but Eden always believed that his hold was a permanent one. I wish to God he'd forget himself and forget women and give his mind to the job. Once in a while, he does—and then I don't have to explain why I hired him. If I ever get near God, which is doubtful, I'll ask Him to reserve His gifts for those who are prepared to make full use of them. You won't talk to Margaret?"

"No."

"I didn't think you would. But I'm a great one for trying." He went away and I began to type. After a time, I heard a curious noise and realised that it was myself humming an old Scottish tune. Astounded, I sat with my hands idle, a wave of happiness flooding over me. I felt as though I had swum with difficulty across a dangerous river and now, standing on the bank, could look back at three figures still struggling in the water: Neil, Eden, Margaret. I was out of it all. I was free.

I heard myself speaking aloud.

"I'm through with them," I said. "No more,"

There was to be a great deal more.

Chapter Four

To Madam's gratification, James Maitland began to form the habit of bringing members of the cast home to lunch, or dinner, or both. They were all, he explained, sick of restaurants. Rehearsals had begun in earnest, and home was the best place in which to relax—but he was the only one of them who had a home in London, or for that matter anywhere else. Christina Hedberg occupied a penthouse near Grosvenor Square; Neil was in a two-roomed flat in Knights-bridge, while Eden and Margaret, who since their marriage had stayed at hotels in whatever town Eden happened to be appearing, were now in service rooms in Chelsea.

The only notice we got of the number expected to meals was James's telephone message to say they were on their way. After some heated sessions with the cook, he came to complain to me.

"What's the matter with the catering in this house?" he demanded. "Isn't there a larder with some spare food in it? Isn't there any canned food for emergencies? Isn't there a spare chop or two to feed to friends?"

"You buy it. We'll serve it." I told him.

We were talking in the study. It was a nice, sunny morning and he was anxious to hurry away to rehearsal, but my words checked him.

"Is Madame short of money?" he asked.

I knew that she was. Since James's arrival, there had been no childhood friends; I had been wondering uneasily whether this was because they didn't want to come while he was here, or whether they didn't want to come. Whatever the reason, our standard of living had been falling fast.

"There's never too much money," I replied cautiously.

"But when I suggested being a paying guest, some time ago, she took umbrage."

"She wouldn't like you to be a paying guest. It would hurt her feelings."

"Never mind about her feelings. She told me to use this house as my home; if I ask guests home to meals, I want to offer them more than cold ham and hot potatoes. Can't you see to it?"

"I'll see to it if you'll pay for it."

"Then start seeing to it now. Stock up the larder with stuff that doesn't need four hours' cooking. You needn't mention the transaction to Madame."

I saw him taking out his wallet, and stopped him.

"There's no need for spot cash," I told him. "I'll open an account in your name. Three accounts, in fact. Stores, meat, fish."

"And talk to the cook. Tell her that I can't give three days' notice every time I want to bring somebody in to a meal."

"Wine?" I inquired as he was going out.

He turned.

"We've been drinking wine. Where's that been coming from?"

"From a wine merchant who refused to supply any more until his bill's paid."

He stood staring at me for a moment or two as if he was going to say something more—then he went out of the room and closed the door behind him.

There was a man, I mused, full of kindly feeling. A hand in his pocket to help his old aunt—to provide food for his guests. *Carte blanche* to his aunt's secretary to buy food and wine—for himself and his guests. I got out the car and drove away to talk to the tradesmen and order his food, and I hoped it would choke him. I didn't want him to concern himself with my affairs, but I felt strongly that it ought to have occurred to him that among his aunt's unpaid bills, there might be one for the secretary's salary.

The change in our social habits took Madame's mind abruptly off her brother's beginnings, and thus I ceased to hear about her own. If these well-known actors and actresses were to come to lunch or to dine, she told me, she must have something to wear. I must drive her to her dressmaker's. I must help her to buy silk for the afternoon and velvet for the evening, and while we were at it, we may as well buy some lengths of tartan to be made up for the visit to Scotland. Clans? Nonsense; she would choose the colours she liked best, and never mind about clans. The bills duly came in, and as they came, I put them into envelopes and placed them on James Maitland's dressing-table.

The meals proved too dull, or Madame proved too much for Christina Hedberg and for the younger members of the cast; soon only Neil and Eden were left. A little later, Margaret was added to the number, and there were six of us round the table.

At meals in the hall of mirrors I could see us all reflected from every angle. I saw Eden's profile and James Maitland's hair—now growing long again at the back—and Margaret's beautiful, level dark eyes and lovely mouth. Madame took the head of the table and James the foot; in order not to have husband and wife sitting together, Eden was placed on Madame's right hand and Neil on her left. Margaret was on James's right; I was on his left, next to Eden. So Eden and I had to engage in polite conversation.

"How are rehearsals going?"

"Pretty well, I think."

"Which theatre will you be appearing in?"

"The Kings," he said—and I wondered if he was remembering his last appearance there.

"Do all the rehearsals take place in London?"

"Most of them. With luck, we'll get two days in the theatre up in Edinburgh—the Monday and the Tuesday. We open on the Wednesday."

Margaret's eyes sometimes rested on us. Neil's eyes seldom left us, but it was impossible to guess what either of them was thinking.

Eden's manner, outwardly composed and polite, still seemed to me to have something of tenseness behind it. I might have put this down to embarrassment arising from the awkwardness of his situation—if I had not known only too well that neither awkwardness nor embarrassment had ever troubled him. My feeling that he wanted to talk to me was soon proved to have some foundation, for one morning he cornered me in the study.

I was standing at the desk, sorting papers. He came in, asked where James was, learnt from me that he was out and Madame not yet down—and then, instead of going away, as I expected, closed the door and came to stand beside me.

"This is the first time I've had a chance to see you alone, Alison. Or perhaps, when the chance has been there, I haven't had the courage to seize it."

"Well, you've seized it now," I pointed out mildly. "What's on your mind?"

"You. Day in and day out. You."

"You shouldn't have seized the chance," I told him. "This is simply a waste of your time and mine."

"I've longed to see you. I've longed to talk to you. I've longed—"

"Look Eden," I broke in as gently as possible, "this really

isn't any use."

"Can you honestly say that you've forgotten the past?" he demanded.

"I can honestly say." I assured him.

"I can't believe that. I've never been able to get you out of my mind, Alison. If I ever hurt you, I'm sorry."

I looked at him. There he was; I could take a long, clear look. I could study the splendid figure, the noble head, the clear-cut features—and also the quiet manner which I had once taken for gentleness, but which I now saw to be an almost frightening insensitiveness. I realised that what Neil had said was true: here was a man incapable of believing that a woman who had loved him could free herself completely from his hold, could move on, move away from him, leave him behind and—most incredible of all—forget him. On his face I could see nothing but the confident certainty that he had only to call and await the inevitable grateful response. I thought suddenly of a rock on the sea's edge, hard, immovable, unchanging whether the water lapped gently at its foot or dashed wildly against its sides.

I came out of my abstraction to find that he had taken one of my hands. I withdrew it.

"I think this had better stop, Eden," I said.

There was a calm finality in my voice that would have carried conviction to most men. But his next words summed up his philosophy.

"I can't believe that you've forgotten me," he said.

Making him believe, I knew, would be almost impossible. If I said quietly that it was all over, it would make no difference. If I became angry, he would think that anger concealed anguish. My only hope was to be brisk. I spoke very briskly indeed.

"I'd love to listen, Eden, honestly I would—but at some other time and in some other place. I've been longing to catch you for a nice, friendly chat about old times, but you know what a panic I always get into when my work falls behind." I even patted his coat sleeve in sisterly apology. "Do run along—or if you'd rather, sit on that nice comfortable chair and wait for James. He's bound to look in; I'm doing some work for him."

If I'd been acting, he would have seen through the act. But my manner—genuinely busy, genuinely anxious to rid myself of an incumbrance—hammered the truth, smashed the truth through layer after layer of vanity and self-love. He had to believe, and the moment of realisation showed clearly in his eyes, ugly and menacing. I had stripped something from him; I could see his hate rising and reaching out towards me.

He stood quite still for some moments, and then he turned and walked to the door and I had an eerie feeling that he was walking blindly, scarcely knowing where he was or what he was doing. He seemed to pause and focus, and then he opened the door and left it swinging behind him and I saw him go across the hall and out of the house.

If either Madame or James Maitland had had what I can only call normal curiosity about any of us, our meals together might have been awkward—but Madame talked about Norway and her brother, and James talked of Paris and Christina Hedberg.

At the end of meals, Madame always rose ceremoniously and led the ladies into the drawing-room; it was inevitable that before long, one of these lunch parties would coincide with Madame's classes. When this day came, she went away, leaving Margaret and myself alone.

Neil had told me more than once how much I had changed. I couldn't see any outward change, but I knew that in the past year and a half I had learnt a great deal. I had become more self-possessed, much more aware of what went on around me, much more wary of its effects on myself. But I hadn't changed in the way Margaret had changed.

To anyone who hadn't known her before her marriage, she must have appeared a tall, slender, rather lifeless beauty. She spoke politely, but without any sign of interest or enthusiasm; she did nothing whatsoever to keep the conversation going. When I looked at her and remembered what she had been less than two years ago, I felt that I was looking at a ship not so much wrecked as beached.

When Madame left us, we looked across the room at one another and for the first time allowed our curiosity full rein. We took stock of all that could be seen and, because we knew one another so well, we saw most of what couldn't be seen. It was she who spoke first.

"Did you come straight to London?"

"Yes."

"Did you have other jobs, or only this one?"

"Only this one. I stayed at a cheap hotel for three or four weeks, looking round, and then I came here."

"What made you pick Madame?"

"She came to the Agency while I was there. She was wearing a long black cloak, and a hat with a large brim and a flat crown; she looked like one of those sherry advertisements. She interviewed me then and there, but she said she wasn't too keen to engage a young girl again, because her last four secretaries had left her to get married. The only thing she wanted to know about me was whether I had anybody in view. I said that I hadn't."

There was a pause. Her face was very pale.

"I wondered where you were," she said. "But I never once thought of London."

"That's what Neil said."

It was my turn to ask questions—but I knew most of what there was to know. She'd married Eden Croft and it hadn't worked out.

"If you'd married him," I heard her say evenly, "I don't think things would have been very different."

I made no reply. The door opened and the three men came in. A swift glance round the room told Eden that Madame was not present, and he addressed Margaret.

"We'd better be off," he said. "We've a lot to do."

Through the open door we could hear, above the waltz accompaniment, Madame's instructions to her class.

One, two three, *down,* two, three, *up,* two, three...

Margaret paused on her way out and spoke to me.

"How about lunch sometime—somewhere else?" She asked.

"I'd like that," I said.

James accompanied them to the front door. I took a cigarette and Neil brought me a light.

"Margaret's left her gloves behind," I said, and nodded towards the sofa.

"I'll take them with me when I go. What have you been saying to Eden?"

"Nothing much. He came in here and made some unconvincing speeches about his feeling for me. I managed to make him see that I wasn't interested. You were right when you mentioned permanent holds. Perhaps he'll settle down now."

"Perhaps he won't. Where are you going?"

"Back to work, of course."

"Why the hell do you let Maitland give you so much to do? He doesn't pay your salary."

"By an indirect process, he does."

James Maitland entered the room and spoke thoughtfully.

"If I had to pick out a happily married young couple," he said, "I wouldn't choose your friends. That girl makes me uneasy. Every time I look at her, I feel that something's boiling inside her. Looking at them both, I feel pretty certain they've just been through some kind of crisis. She looks as though she's searching for a weapon. Not that it's any of my business."

"A weapon?" repeated Neil.

"That's what I said. If anything happens to hurt a woman like that, I imagine she likes to hurt back. If I were her husband, I'd watch out. She could be dangerous."

"Wrong again," I said.

"No, he's right," said Neil. "That is, he's right in general even if he's wrong about Margaret. And don't start that I've-known-her-all-my-life chant. You proved last year that having known her all your life, you knew nothing whatsoever about her."

I felt too angry to speak. I walked towards the door with the intention of going to the study, but James Maitland barred the way.

"Look now," he protested mildly. "No quarrels. We've got to be a team."

"You go ahead and be a team," I said. "I'm going to get on with my job."

"Time enough. Neil and I want to talk to you about Madame. Is she quite determined to come up to Edinburgh?"

"Why shouldn't she go up to Edinburgh?" I asked. "It's her brother's play. You want to fill the theatre, don't you?"

"She's talked too much to the Press down here," Neil said. "Nobody can stop her from going up to Edinburgh, but perhaps you can stop her from getting into the foreground of all the news pictures. She's beginning to draw the attention of the crowds—like the Queen of Tonga at the Coronation. That would be all right if this play were a comedy, but it isn't. It's a tragedy, and she just doesn't go with the sombre setting. We don't want a joker in the pack."

I thought suddenly of Madame's tartan outfit, made specially for the journey to Scotland. Wearing it, she was going to look like a combination of Rob Roy and Harry Lauder. I laughed.

"Why don't you get her into the cast," I said. "She'd act the others off the stage—Eden and all."

"Thank you," Neil said. "She's enough trouble out of the cast." He turned to James. "What did you do with those designs for the second act?" he asked.

James didn't know what he'd done with the designs and it took some time for me to convince him that he had not given them to me.

"Well, if that's the case," he said, "they must be up in my room. I'll go up and get them."

He went out and shut the door; Neil and I were left alone.

"Will you come out to dinner with me tonight?" he asked.

The question came with such abruptness that for some seconds I could only stare at him.

"What's the matter?" he asked. "Don't you eat? Or don't you like the idea of appearing in public with a sinister-looking escort like myself. Or do you want ten days' notice? Or do you have to ask Madame's permission?"

"No. No permission; it's after hours."

"Then will you come?"

"Yes," I heard myself saying to my own astonishment. "Yes, I will."

"You're full of surprises," he said.

"So are you. What time?"

"Eight for eight-thirty, as your godmother used to say and probably still does." He came and stood beside me. "Four and a half hours," he said.

"To do what?"

"To wait."

He put out a hand, pulled me to him, and bent and put his lips on mine for a long, hard moment.

We both heard the door open. Neil released me slowly and unhurriedly and we turned, expecting to see James. He was there, but in front of him stood Eden.

Nobody spoke. Eden looked round, walked into the room, picked up Margaret's gloves and held them up for an instant.

"I came back for these," he said.

He went out without a glance at any of us and without another word. James, after watching him going out of the house, turned to us and spoke reflectively.

"He didn't seem to like your little exhibition of auld lang syne," he commented. "Now he'll treat us all to more manifestations of temperament."

84

"Let's go," was all Neil said, and flung a passing remark over his shoulder at me. "Eight o'clock. I was thinking of borrowing Eden's car, but I've changed my mind; we'll use taxis."

I went slowly into the study and sat down at my desk, feeling, if anything, a sense of relief. If Eden had wanted further proof, he had seen it when he had opened the door. Whether it was a good thing to go out to dinner with Neil or not, I didn't know, but something told me that going would take me a long step away from Eden and I was certain that that was a very good thing indeed.

I wore a green dress for dinner. An old dress. If Neil remembered it, he gave no sign. We got into a taxi; it had been raining, and the streets were wet and glistening; I looked out at all the gleaming reflections and wondered how anybody could dislike rain.

"Where are we going?" I asked.

"To a place which will be full of actors and actresses who've always wondered whether there was anything the matter with me because they've never seen me out with a woman. The food will be good, though a little over-elaborate, and we'll talk about the past. But not the recent past. I remembered something odd the other day: my first realisation that there was a strange girl living in Margaret's house. My parents told me that your parents were dead. The idea was to make me feel sorry for you, but all I felt was envy."

"Could somebody have removed your parents' little boy and put you in his place?" I asked. "Nobody ever had nicer parents than yours; how else can you explain the fact that you never got on with them?"

"I think it was those Scottish Sundays. They are, after all, a pious pair. Sundays... My God! I can still feel those collars. But if you protest to pious parents against going to church, they get to work trying to save your soul. Perhaps that accounts for it all. I think your godmother saw how things were going; I think she would have helped me, if I'd let her. But in those days I didn't realise what I felt about her; in fact, I didn't realise that I felt anything at all about her until I saw her after you left home."

The car stopped outside a dimly-lit restaurant. Inside was even dimmer lighting, which suggested that the actors and actresses didn't want to see too much of one another. We were led deferentially to a corner table and given menus. Neil reached across the table and took mine away.

"I'll order" he said. "Women like you used to choose the lowest prices; now they look for the lowest calories."

I enjoyed the meal. Throughout it, Neil talked, and talked very well. I had never before seen his agreeable side—but however amiable he sounded, nothing seemed to soften the harsh outlines of his face. There must, I felt, be an element of fear in the minds of all who had dealings with him; he had the look of a man who when roused would stop at nothing.

We said good night outside Madame's front door. He took my hand and held it lightly and looked down at me. "Well, thanks" he said. "I enjoyed the evening."

"So did I."

So I had. But in spite of it or because of it, I went up to bed feeling depressed. I realised that I was beginning to look at the three of them—Margaret and Eden and Neil—in a new light. They were beginning to make me feel uneasy—but it wasn't for myself. I was worried on James Maitland's account. His future was, in a sense, in their hands. The crisis had probably arisen out of Margaret's arrival in London; perhaps Eden had asked her to go back to Scotland, and she had refused. If things got any worse between them, if Margaret left him—not to wait for him in Edinburgh, but for good—nobody could tell how Eden would react.

Lying in bed, staring up at the ceiling, I wondered uneasily what kind of trouble lay ahead and reflected that if and when it came, there was no need for me to be mixed up in it. A loving welcome awaited me at home; I had only to give notice to Madame and in a month I could be on my way north, leaving Eden and Margaret and Neil Patterson and James Maitland—and looming trouble—behind. I'd had more than my share eighteen months ago; I didn't feel like risking any more.

Looking back over the years, I seemed to see the chart of my life—a slight downward curve in the early years, marking the death of my parents; between that and my twenty-fourth year an almost level line. Nobody could have had a happier life than I'd had until I was twenty-four; perhaps this had been a poor preparation for dealing with trouble when it came, but it had given me something to fall back on, something to pull on, something to hold on to, something to grasp in the long climb back.

I was back where I wanted to be. I was living the life I had once lived—quiet, uneventful, perhaps even dull—but a life that suited me. I didn't want to get involved with Neil and Eden again. I would have liked to meet Margaret on something like our old terms, but it did not seem likely that either of us could cross the barrier that Eden had erected.

I don't know how long I lay thinking things over. I think I would have chosen the safe way out and told Madame on the following morning that I was leaving—if I hadn't remembered that in her and in her nephew I had two perfect examples of how to live one's own life and let other people live theirs. I could at least try to learn from them. I could study the science of detachment. There was no need to cut short my last weeks with Madame; I would work for her until we went up to Edinburgh for the Festival and then, my job over, I would go home. If the play was a success, if Eden was a success, so much the better; if not, it wasn't my problem and there was no risk of my becoming involved.

It was Robert Burns who pointed out that the best-laid schemes o' mice an' men gang aft a-gley. It was too late to ask him why he left out women.

Chapter Five

Madame was getting ready for the road; she had bought thermos flasks in three sizes, a fitted picnic hamper, a folding picnic table and, for herself, a stout—very stout—camp stool.

James brought the bills to me and waved them angrily in my face.

"Were you with Madame when she bought all this trash?" he demanded.

"Yes, I was."

"You just stood by and let her do it?"

"Not exactly. I expostulated."

"Oh, you did? Well, you can send all the things back to wherever they came from and explain that she's changed her mind about going on safari. Haven't you explained to her that it's only four hundred miles from London to Edinburgh?"

"Several times."

"I dare say as you're driving that hearse of hers, you'll have to spend a night on the road—but not necessarily *on* the road. I'm surprised she didn't buy herself a tent and a sleeping-bag."

"She wants to take the trip slowly, picnicking all the way."

"Well, let her. The rest of us haven't got time for sylvan sports; we'll just go on driving."

If the weather hadn't been so perfect during the first weeks of August, that's what we would have done. But the sun shone, London sweltered and the advantages of a leisurely trip became more and more obvious. It would, James decided at last, be an ideal way of providing a break between hard work in London and harder work in Edinburgh. I would drive Madame, he would take Christina, while Neil, who had no car, could go by train or air or accompany us and shuttle from Eden's to Madame's car as the fancy took him.

"This is just what I advised in the first place" said Madame. "This is just what I said. Why should we not enjoy the countryside? I shall make a time-table saying when we shall start and where we shall go. It is better always to have everything planned. We shall all enjoy ourselves and become very healthy."

It would be new ground for Madame and James, for neither of them had seen Scotland. My own feeling was that it was going to be a very ill-assorted party, and as I knew Margaret disliked motor tours I was curious to hear what she thought of the plan. But asking her was difficult, for since our brief exchange when we had been alone in the drawing-room, she had not been to the house, and the invitation to lunch with her had not been renewed.

We met by chance one morning in Harrods, waiting by

the lifts. She wanted to go up, I was going down. She was wearing a striped cotton dress and a big, floppy-brimmed, absurd, heavenly straw hat.

"Hello, Margaret."

She looked from me to the ascending lift; it stopped and the door slid open, but instead of stepping into it, she moved away.

"Are you in a hurry?" she asked me.

"No."

"Coffee?"

"Why not?"

As we sat at our table, I asked her what she thought of the plans for driving up to the Festival.

"It's better than rushing up there," she said. "If we don't do it this way, we'll do it non-stop and I can't bear driving with Eden when he's in a hurry. Just so long as I don't ever have to travel in the same car as Madame, I'll be able to stand it."

"Why do you dislike her so much? She's eccentric, but she's harmless and good natured."

"Harmless perhaps; good natured, no. If you could strip off that facade of fat, you'd find a tiger underneath. Have you told her you're leaving?"

"Not yet."

"She'll lash her tail. Alison—"

I waited, but there seemed to be no more.

"We were going to meet—and talk," I reminded her.

91

"What made you change your mind?"

"Eden heard me asking you out to lunch. He didn't like it. If he's to keep his mind on his work..."

"I see," I said.

"I thought that if we could wait until later, until we met at home...."

"I'll do anything you want me to do."

"It isn't only the play that's important. This is Eden's last chance—on the stage and off. If he walks out of this part, Neil's through with him—and so am I. So it seems fairer, for the moment, to do what he wants."

There seemed to be nothing more to say. We sat on in silence, the coffee untouched on the table in front of us, and I knew that what she had just said was only partly true. Success at Edinburgh might keep Neil and Eden together, but for Margaret, the end was in sight.

I went home feeling that although we had said little, the meeting had left her lighter in spirit. On the following morning, I recalled her opinion of Madame, for when I said that I would not be coming back to London after the Festival, the tail lashed indeed.

At first Madame didn't believe me. She simply stared at me across the breakfast tray, her eyes wide and astonished.

"Ah, I see," she said at last on a note of relief. "You wish for a holiday. Well this you must have. I forgot that so long a time had passed since you came to me. When I engaged you, we didn't agree anything about holidays, did we?"

"No, Madame. But it isn't a holiday I want. I shall hate leaving you, and I can't tell you how grateful I am for all you've done—but it's time I went home."

"Home?" There was a faint edge on her voice. "But you have no home."

"I'm going back to my godmother."

"She is old? She has asked you to go and look after her?"

"No. She has two maids who are devoted to her—but I've been away a long time and I want to go back."

"And how about myself?" demanded Madame. "Am I to be left?"

"That's why I wanted to tell you now," I said. "I thought that before going up to Scotland, you could interview some girls and choose one of them to replace me."

"How could you think that? You know how busy I am. You know that at this time I am doing something from morning to night. I was looking forward very much to this journey, but now you want to rob me of this pleasure. How can I have any enjoyment when I know that my life is to be disorganised, my future plans upset? At my age, one does not easily make changes. It is a great shock to hear suddenly like this that you are not happy and wish to go."

"I'm very happy, Madame."

"You have got yourself other work?"

"No, Madame. I'll look for a job up in Scotland."

"Then if you are leaving me in this way," she said angrily, "you are very ungrateful. When you came to me, you were thin and ill. Now you are still thin but you are healthy. I fed you well, I looked after you, I made you—you said yourself—happy. For this, perhaps you owe me a little consideration."

I thought for a moment of promising to stay until she had found a suitable successor—but I didn't make the offer. Something told me that if I did, it would be a long, long time before I got away. I spoke as gently as I could.

"I'm very grateful indeed to you, Madame. But I owe my godmother something, too."

"When I interviewed you in that Agency, you were, one could see, not happy. Why did you not go to your godmother then?"

"There were very good reasons, Madame."

"Then there are even better ones why you should not go now. You have been with me a long time. You are used to me, I am used to you. You have stayed longer than any other girl. Am I to have a new person now, while James is here and my house is full of guests? Am I to be obliged to teach a new girl, train a new girl?"

"If you would let me speak to the Agency," I said, "they would send up girls today, if you wanted them to. If you engaged someone now, she could work with me until we left for Scotland and—"

"—and then what?" broke in Madame. "Am I to leave

this strange girl here alone? Am I to pay her to stay here doing nothing? Am I to leave a stranger here for the cook to feed, for the cleaning women to work for? No, this does not suit me. You must think more about this."

"I'm sorry, Madame," I began. "I—"

"I will not speak about this now," she broke in. "I have a tiring day in front of me, and you have upset me very much. I would not have said that you could have done this to me. I think that I made a mistake when I treated you as my own family, when I introduced you to my friends and included you with my guests and treated you as my daughter instead of as my secretary."

"Secretary-companion," I put in quietly.

"I think you are very selfish to have told me this at such a time when I was so happy." Her voice rose. "I think it is wicked of you to spoil my pleasure in this way."

I found myself, to my dismay, in partial agreement with this statement. Perhaps it would have been kinder to have waited; in thinking about myself, I had forgotten her. It would have been kinder to have come back from Edinburgh with her and stayed with her for a little while after James's departure. She was going to miss him very much. I thought of saying something of this to her, but her next words changed my mood.

"I have always known that you would do something like this," she said. "Outside, you have always been calm and polite—but underneath, I have always said to myself that you are sly. Something happened to you before you came to work for me; this I have always known. One could see. But it was not my business, so I did not inquire. It did not interest me; I have my own life to lead. But now I think that you must have got yourself into some kind of trouble. It would have been wiser if I had made more inquiries about you." Her hands were trembling. Her eyes, glaring at me across the room, looked malevolent, and she was clearly preparing to say more in the same vein. I turned quietly and went out of the room.

James Maitland came into the study half an hour later and closed the door firmly behind him.

"Well, what's it all about?" he asked. "Madame sent for me. She's still in her dressing-gown, walking up and down her bedroom breathing noisily and looking as though she's about to launch into an aria."

"I told her I was leaving. She didn't like it."

"Well, who would? You're a pretty efficient secretary. Why did you spring it on her like this ?"

"There was no spring about it. One has to give a reasonable amount of notice. I thought if I told her now, she'd interview a few girls and pick out one I could train, one I could make just as useful as I am. But she wouldn't hear of it. I'm sorry she's upset. I'm upset too. I like her; I've been happy here; she's done a lot for me. She's done more than she knows. But everything has to come to an end, hasn't it?"

"Why do you want to go home suddenly?"

"It isn't suddenly. I've been here nearly two years."

"But surely London's a better place to work in than Edinburgh?"

"What makes you think so?"

"There's more money down here, for one thing. You meet more people; you get more variety. Home's home and everyone who's got a home wants to go there now and again, but surely you don't want to shut yourself up with an old woman? You're shut up with one here, but at least you've got London at your door."

"I want to go home," I said.

"I heard you. Nobody's going to try and stop you from going home. All I'm suggesting is that you go home while you're up in Edinburgh, see your godmother, spend some time with her and then come back to Madame and ease yourself out of this job gradually. She knows that you can't stay with her for ever. You'll marry, for one thing. Next time you tell her you're leaving, invent some fellow up in Scotland and pretend you're going to marry him."

"Stranger things have happened."

"You said yourself that you liked to see Madame having a good time. Tell her you'll stay on a bit longer. Tell her you'll come back here with her."

"No, I won't. I almost did, when I saw that she was upset at my leaving—but she said too much."

"She's old and you made her angry. Angry old ladies do say too much; it's a habit they fall into."

"She said I was in some sort of trouble when she engaged me."

"I daresay she'll overlook it. Were you in trouble?"

"Yes, but not the kind she meant."

"Well, I'll tell her that I've persuaded you to think it over. For one thing, if you don't come back to London, who's going to drive that car of Madame's back?"

I was annoyed to realise that I'd forgotten all about the car. Remembering it, I also recalled another fact: that tomorrow was Madame's birthday. I had indeed chosen a bad moment for breaking my news.

Watching my expression, James Maitland pursued his advantage.

"You see? You haven't considered the thing in all its aspects. I'll go up and tell Madame that you've relented, and then she'll get dressed and come down and apologise to you."

"I don't want her to apologise, and it isn't a question of relenting. I want to go home."

"Careful. It's becoming an obsession."

He went away, returned to tell me that Madame had agreed to keep me on after all, and then told me to put my work aside.

"You're coming out for a nice walk. I'll take you twice round the Park. Bring some bread and we'll feed the ducks."

Walking with him meant sprinting to keep up with his seven-league strides. While he fed the ducks, I rested my feet and regained my breath. On the way home, he chose books and ordered flowers for Madame while I bought her a blue bed-jacket. When we got back to the house, I was winded but refreshed.

He turned back from the door to go and buy some cigarettes. I went into the study; to my surprise, Christina Hedberg was seated on a low chair, her feet dangling comfortably over the arms.

"Hello," she said amiably.

She had not been amiable on our first two or three meetings, but after careful scrutiny, had decided that there was no competition.

"Go ahead and work if you want to," she invited in English that had a strong American flavour. "Don't take any notice of me. I'm just sitting here waiting for James."

I typed swiftly, but for once inaccurately. I was comparing her with Margaret. There were wide differences, but there were likenesses too. They were both beautiful; they both had that air of ease and confidence that you see in women who are rich and sought-after; they both invariably had a small fortune on their backs. But Margaret's clothes were quiet, conventional; she could look as casual as anybody, but she still looked groomed. This girl was of the type my godmother once called, dispassionately, the new slut. Everything she had on had cost a mint, but her shoes looked scruffy, her sweater was five times too large and her slacks four sizes too small. Her hair was expensively arranged to look as though nothing had been done to it for weeks.

"You like this work?" she inquired, as I paused to insert a fresh sheet of paper into the typewriter.

"Yes, very much."

"You are so pretty—you do not find all this a waste of your time?"

"I get paid for doing it."

Lifting one lovely shoulder contemptuously, she dismissed my salary.

"I could not live like you. No girl has to, while there are men."

"Men with money," I amended, and went on typing with the feeling that the conversation wasn't really getting us anywhere. A splendid young lioness on the prowl, stopping to exchange a word with a contented she-bear, would probably have said very much what we were saying now.

I was relieved when James came in. Neil came with him—and although I couldn't observe the slightest outward change in Christina, I knew that with the entrance of the two men, she had changed gear. Whatever interest she had had in me was extinguished.

"You two girls been having a nice chat?" James inquired blandly.

"Never mind about the chat," Neil broke in, his voice and manner irritable. "Christina, who's this Oskar-with-a-K fellow who's trailing you?"

"He is Prince Oskar. He is—"

"He's cluttering up rehearsals. If he can't keep away from you, keep him away from the theatre."

Without another word, he turned and walked out of the room and banged the door behind him.

"Pleasant chap," James said reflectively.

"He is an ugly black devil," Christina said, swinging her legs to the floor and looking with narrowed angry eyes at the door out of which Neil had just gone. "You know something? When I hesitated to decide about this part, it was because of the things I heard about Eden Croft. But I would rather work with Croft than with Patterson."

I saw James's eyes resting speculatively on her.

"I find it hard to discover exactly why Croft had to wait so long before getting a part like this one" he said.

"What they told me was that he's a good actor, but he doesn't agree with the basic principle of drama: that the show must go on. If a man doesn't believe in that, he oughtn't to be acting. Off stage, we all know, actors are free to do just what they want to do; actresses, too. But once we get our cue, we've got to get on-stage and act. The show must go on. But Croft has shown over and over again that he doesn't care whether the show goes on or comes off. When I learned this I took it up with Patterson and we had it out. He came over to Paris to see me, and swore that this time, Croft would give a magnificent performance and give it as long as we need it. So on that, I agreed to take the part—and now I find Croft easy and Neil impossible. You will have to speak to him seriously, James."

She got to her feet, stubbed out her cigarette in my ashtray and spoke with all the authority of her fame.

"Madame asked me to lunch. Please tell her that I am unable to come without the Prince, so I will bring him with me.

James accompanied her to the front door and came back to the study.

"The social hour's over," I said.

"This is business. Were you ever engaged to Patterson?"

"No.

"That's hard to believe. When he's with you, he has the air of a discarded lover. He lives near your godmother, I understand."

"Yes."

"What's your godmother like?"

"Tall and gracious."

"Does she look anything like Margaret?"

"In old photographs, yes."

He seemed to be calculating.

"You haven't, as far as I can gather, much money and Margaret appears to have a great deal. That must have made difficulties for your godmother."

"It didn't make difficulties for anybody. She sent Margaret and myself to the same school; then we had a sort of family conference and my godmother gave me a choice: to go on with Margaret to a finishing school, or to go to a secretarial school on my own. I chose the secretarial school."

"Why couldn't she have finished you both together and then held the family conference?"

"Because it was clear, even then, that Margaret and I were going different ways. It wasn't only that she was a rich woman's daughter and I only had a moderate income of my own; she and I were as close as sisters in one way, but poles apart in others. I'm the office type; the only exercise I like is walking and swimming. She's crazy about riding and tennis and golf and skiing, and she does them all at championship level. She can even shoot."

"So she went shooting and you went to the secretarial school. And then?"

"And then I got a job. I got it all on my own. I remember going home and telling my godmother about it; I nearly burst with pride."

"And then?"

"More jobs—until I got this one. Do you mind if I get on with it?"

"There's no hurry."

I was getting used to this phrase and the way in which he uttered it. He made it sound the very essence of leisure. Listening, you really felt that there was no hurry. No hurry at all.

"I want to ask you something else," he was saying. "About Croft's wife. About Margaret."

"Well?"

"She's by any standards attractive—agreed?"

"Yes."

"In fact, you could call her beautiful."

"You could."

"And she's rich. I gather that at present, she and Eden are limping along on what her father left her—an income I myself would call sizeable—but she's her rich mamma's only child-right?"

"Right."

"So that she could, as they say, have married anybody; that's to say, she could have taken her pick. So what does she do? She marries Croft. I've got reasonable eyesight, but I can't see that he's got anything to recommend him but his looks. I can't detect any one factor, apart from the way he looks, that could make him acceptable as a husband to any woman as sensitive, as sensible, as intelligent as Margaret appears to be. So what's the secret? Secret there must be—and only women seem able to read it; women of all ages and types. You seem to be safely encased in your ice pack, but look at Margaret, look at Madame; look even at Christina. If Croft lifted a finger, she'd forego all her other commitments and settle for him."

"There's no secret. As a man, you can't be expected to feel another man's—"

"Feel, no. And I'm not talking about my feelings. Don't run away with the idea that I care. I'm a great gawk and if I want any woman to notice me, I have to work at it—but Croft just stands there and catches them as they fall. How does he achieve this extraordinary success?"

"Achieve? Achieve means success after effort—and as you've just acknowledged, there's no effort. There's no deception, either; he doesn't pretend to have any special qualities. The deception is all on the other side—the woman's side. He likes women. He's at his best with women. He makes an evening with him memorable because it's clear that he's enjoyed every moment of it. His voice is so musical that it doesn't really matter much what he says; his manner is gentle; you can't fault him on clothes or food or wine. He's not amusing, but he's willing to be amused. When he's with a woman, he's completely absorbed in her, and it's not his fault if she makes the mistake of thinking that she's the only one who can hold his attention. A woman has to know him for a long time, or get away from him altogether, before the cracks become noticeable."

I stopped. In the silence that followed, I saw James Maitland regarding me curiously.

"So that's it," he said slowly at last.

My hands weren't too steady. I pulled out a drawer and handed him a sheaf of bills.

"Madame's," I said. "Can you let me have a cheque?"

He looked through them; as I had hoped, they effected an abrupt change in his train of thought.

"When is she going to stop?" he demanded.

"It's your own fault. You told her she was going to have a

share of the profits, and she's having them."

"She's mortgaging her share and my share too. Have you looked lately at all those food bills?"

"You're entertaining people in your own home—isn't that what you said? And now you've got a Prince to feed."

"And a genuine one at that," he said morosely. "I can't remember his full credentials, but he's another one of Queen Victoria's great-great-greats. See what I mean by having to work hard for a woman's attention? I thought I was making progress with Christina. She's been helping me to choose a car; she picked on one that's fast, with blue cushions. If my luck holds and this Prince can be by-passed and she agrees to drive up to Edinburgh with me, I'll go by road, passing you and Madame on the way. It's a nice, cosy car; you press a button and the hood comes down, and there's Christina all blonde against the blue. It ought to be good publicity as well as good fun."

"Nobody'll give a second glance at her or at you; attention's going to be riveted on Madame in her North-of-the-Border outfit. She's got a little hat with a blackcock's feather, and brogues, and a shooting-stick. And yesterday, she bought a cairngorm."

"A—? Oh yes, I know."

"Are you sure you know?"

"Quite sure. I've been reading it all up."

"Scotland?"

"Edinburgh. I haven't got hold of its geography yet, but I've learnt about its golden age, when the men of Edinburgh looked upon Londoners as barely civilized."

"Which they still do."

"They didn't feel so superior before Walter Scott got to work and aroused all that national feeling. Do you know what Voltaire said?"

"Of course I know. He said that the rules of taste in all the arts, from epic poems to gardening, came from Scotland. And he was right. And now would you mind very much if I got on with the job I'm being paid to do?"

He rose and went to the door but I stopped him.

"The cheque."

He wrote it and put it on the table.

"My book said that the Scots were a thrifty race. Perhaps you'd inculcate a little thrift into Madame?"

"Soon. But not just yet. She's having a good time; let her enjoy it."

"It needn't be entirely at my expense. The cook's been hinting that Madame has other male means of support."

"Never mind about them," I said. "They're childhood friends."

"Speaking of childhood friends, I've lost my umbrella again. Could you go and get it from the Wings and Flies?"

"I give notice that this is positively the last time. What's the Wings and Flies—a pub?"

107

"Not a pub—a club. Theatrical club. It's in Wardour Street; I don't know the number, but it's above that little shop that sells surgical appliances horrid to behold. You go up four flights—I'm sorry there's no lift; you knock on a green door and a fellow called Joe will give you the umbrella, if it's there. I'm pretty sure it's there. I've got some letters, by the way. If you're not back, I'll leave them on the desk."

I drove to the Wings and Flies Club and walked up the four flights of stairs. There was no umbrella. It had been taken away, Joe said, by a gentleman named Mr. Neil Patterson, who had promised to deliver it to the owner.

There was no opportunity, before lunch, to tell James Maitland what I thought about this waste of my morning; when I returned to the house, voices in the drawing-room informed me that the visitors had arrived.

There were six of us round the table at lunch: Madame and James, Christina and the Prince, Neil and I. The Prince, to everybody's surprise, turned out to be an admirer of everything Scottish; by the end of lunch, this included me. He was short, stout, middle-aged and rich-looking, and appeared completely impervious to the low temperatures caused by the disproportionate amount of attention he paid to me.

It was not a successful meal. At the end of it, Christina swept her friend away and Madame retired to her room. Neil, still in the irritable mood he had displayed throughout the morning, asked me if I would dine with him on the following evening, and I refused, giving Madame's birthday as an excuse. When the reverberations from his treatment of the front door had died down, I asked James Maitland what his birthday plans were.

"I talked to Madame," he said. "She's asked some friends to lunch, but she wants to add some friends of mine."

"How many altogether?"

"We made it ten."

"How about dinner?"

"She wants me to take her out to dinner and on to a show. Will you fix the menu for lunch and get the theatre tickets?"

"Which show?"

"Nothing with music and nothing funny and nothing in the experimental stage, and nothing historical unless its Shakespeare. See to it, will you?"

I said that I would and he went away. I drove to the shops with a list of special delicacies which I knew Madame would enjoy for lunch; then I bought the theatre tickets and went home. Alone at teatime with James, I submitted the menu for his approval.

"Never," he said, handing it back, "speak to me again of Scottish thrift."

"It's a special occasion," I reminded him.

For me, it proved to be a very special occasion indeed.

Chapter Six

It happened without any kind of warning.

The speaking-tube system throughout the house was old-fashioned, but it worked. The only occasions on which it didn't work was when the cook wasn't at the receiving end.

As she always told us when she was leaving the house, her failure to respond meant that she was in her own flat. She lived in the basement and rarely came upstairs, but there was nothing gloomy or uncomfortable about her quarters; by carrying down the furniture from the unused servants' rooms at the top of the house, as well as a selection of curtains and carpets given to her by Madame, she had made the empty still-room and butler's pantry and servants' hall into a snug little flat for herself. As she made a point of never answering bells, the only way to communicate with her in the flat was either by going all the way downstairs, or—and this method I had invented for myself—by leaning precariously over the banisters in the hall, twisting sideways and pulling a string I had myself attached to the door of her sitting-room. It was a dangerous proceeding, because I had to lean so far over that recovering my balance was difficult—but the fact that it was so dangerous made the cook, who was fond of me, come at once, fearing for my life.

On the morning of Madame's birthday, I pushed my luck too far. I had laid the lunch table and decorated it myself. The flowers looked beautiful; the white wine was cooling; the guests were assembled in the drawing-room. The only trouble was the cook, who, having chased a mouse from refuge to refuge, had finally seen it disappearing into her sitting-room. She cleared out most of the furniture in order to provide fewer hiding-places, and every second that she could spare from the saucepans and the sauces was spent mouse-hunting. I wanted her urgently and the speaking-tube was dead and so I used the banister method—for the last time. I leaned over and reached for the string—and then I knew that I was going to fall. It wasn't a question of overbalancing. The banisters simply gave way.

Bent almost double as I was, the only thing I could do was dive. I dived straight for the stone floor a long way below me, and if there hadn't been a mouse in the kitchen that morning, nothing could have saved me. But instead of breaking my neck on the unyielding stone, I landed on the furniture that the cook had pushed outside her flat—a neatly-arranged circle of a sofa and two big armchairs.

When I was able to take notice again, I found myself in the drawing-room. It had taken three men, James told me, to get me up the stairs; he thought I must have very big bones. When I had recovered a little, I begged them to go to lunch and leave me by myself; when they'd gone, I managed to get upstairs to my own room.

After lunch, Margaret came up to see me. I was lying on my bed and she stood looking anxiously at me.

"All right?" she asked.

"A bit bruised; nothing else. At least, I don't think so."

"Madame was coming up to see you, but I said I'd come instead. She's sent for the doctor."

"She needn't have done. I'm all right."

She sat on the end of the bed and looked a little helplessly at me; in emergency, she was apt to await instructions.

"Are you sure you feel all right? You fell a long way."

"These are high ceilings. Did it cast a gloom on the lunch party?"

"On the contrary. We all had a good time talking about our own narrow escapes from death by disease or drowning."

She spoke lightly, but there was something in her manner that I recognized—a tension that had indicated, in the past, that she was about to tell me, or ask me, something of special importance. She never imparted any news directly; there was always a prelude quite unconnected with whatever was coming—and then she would swerve without warning to what she really wanted to say. Now I saw that it was on her tongue.

"Alison—"

I did my best to show nothing of the shaft of agony that drove through my shoulder, but it was enough to check her. She broke off abruptly.

"I'm crazy," she said gently. "You must be feeling like death."

"It comes and goes. Don't stop talking, Margaret. And don't worry about choosing safe subjects; let's talk as we used to talk. What happened, happened, but we don't have to let it string out for the rest of our lives, do we?"

"It isn't over," she said. "It's still going on. You always over-simplified, Alison."

"All I'm saying"—I paused to ease my aching limbs—"all I'm saying is that—"

What I was saying couldn't be said just then, for we heard Madame's voice outside the door, and a moment later she entered with the doctor. He was a man well into his sixties, short and stout, and he had, I think, mistaken his vocation; he could have been, he should have been, a comedian and not a doctor—but he enjoyed being both.

Madame looked expectantly at Margaret, but Margaret, at a signal from me, stayed where she was.

"Well, well, well." The doctor stood looking down at me jovially. "Attempted suicide isn't my job, you know; it's a matter for the police."

"I told her very often, doctor," said Madame. "I warned her that it was dangerous, but she would do it. If the cook hadn't put those chairs there, what would have happened ?"

"Broken neck," said the doctor cheerfully. "Well, let's take a look at you."

He didn't tell me anything I didn't know already. I was shaken and bruised, but there was nothing broken.

"Give yourself a rest before you make the next attempt," he advised. "This sort of thing is what makes the doctor's fortune—he has to treat one patient for bruises and half a dozen others for shock."

"The cook had hysterics," Madame said, when she had stopped laughing at this sally. "What a time to choose! Just before my birthday lunch."

She patted my arm in a motherly fashion; yesterday's interview might never have been.

"Well, stay where you are today," the doctor said. "And don't get tired of life yet—there's worse to come. I went to see a fellow last week who didn't seem to be making much effort to survive. 'If I live, doc,' he said to me, 'I shan't have money enough to pay your bill; if I die, somebody else will have to take care of it!' Ha ha ha ha ha!"

He and Madame went, shaking, out of the room and I answered Margaret's raised eyebrows.

"His patients die laughing," I explained.

"Madame didn't say anything about food or drink. Can I get you anything?"

"I could do with a nice hot cup of coffee."

"I'll get you one."

She went to the door and I stopped her.

"Margaret—"

She turned and waited.

"You were going to tell me something."

She stood still, saying nothing. Watching her, I saw—saw without believing—an expression on her face that was close to fear. It seemed to me a long time before she answered.

"Whatever it was," she said quietly, "it'll keep."

She opened the door, but before she could close it again, I saw James Maitland in the doorway.

"Can I come in?" he asked.

"Yes, do."

He sat where Margaret had been sitting.

"It was a good lunch," he said. "Pity you missed it."

"I put the theatre tickets in your room. Did you get them?"

"Yes, thanks."

"Have all the visitors gone?"

"All gone. I drove Christina back to her hotel. I sounded her about driving up to Scotland with me, and she seemed to think she would."

"What about Oskar-with-a-K?"

"Him? He carries too much weight, and he's out of condition. Did you remember to book a table for Madame and myself for dinner?"

"How could I book a table? I didn't know where you wanted to dine."

"Patterson took me to a new place in Soho; we'll probably

115

go there. Did you have time to finish those letters before you dived over the banisters?"

"Yes, I did."

"How are you feeling?"

"Thanks for remembering to ask. I'm all right."

I really thought I was, but a shock is a shock and to my horror, I felt tears beginning to roll slowly down my cheeks. James looked at them with a sort of dispassionate interest.

"That's a nice, healthy reaction," he commented. "It'll do you good."

I groped for a handkerchief.

"Do you mind going away?" I asked.

By way of answer, he unfolded his own handkerchief and handed it to me.

"Use that and keep on crying," he said. "It does a girl good to break down now and again."

I didn't seem able to stop, so I turned and pushed my head into the pillow and made a session of it. Margaret came in during the mopping-up operations.

"I made her cry purposely" James said with some pride. "She looks better, doesn't she?" He took the coffee and held it out to me. "Here, drink this."

I drank it and Margaret took the empty cup.

"I've got to go," she said. "Eden went long ago; Neil wanted a lift."

James opened the door for her, closed it again and came

back to the bed. He shook up my pillows and I half-lay, half-sat against them, feeling considerably better.

"A nice girl, Margaret," he said. "Somebody ought to have stopped her from marrying Croft. Didn't anybody try?"

"No," I said, "Nobody tried."

"Not even her mother? From what I gathered from all you didn't say, her mother seems a good, sensible kind of woman. Surely she wasn't taken in by Croft's profile?"

"Margaret was twenty-five."

"An age at which some girls have accumulated a little horse sense. Did she live at home?"

"No. I did, Margaret didn't."

"Where did Margaret live?"

"Oh ... Rome, Paris. She liked to travel."

"And you didn't?"

"I got as far as one can get with a fortnight's holiday a year. And before you go too far astray, I'd like to point out that your picture of Margaret as the lucky one and myself as the foundling is completely wide of the mark. If I'd wanted money or travel or leisure, I could have had it. I only had to ask."

I closed my eyes to indicate that I wasn't in a mood, or in a condition, for reminiscence, but James Maitland was impervious to hints.

"You're all pretty hard to place," he said reflectively. "There's you and Margaret and this tall and gracious god-mother, and then there's Patterson, a childhood friend."

"He wasn't a childhood friend. His parents lived near us and they were great friends of my godmother's. They were nice people; they didn't deserve an only child like Neil. We didn't see much of him, because he was never the social type and anyhow he was always away at school. He spent his holidays keeping himself to himself. When we did meet, we quarrelled. He always looked as he does now: Napoleon-on-the-way-to-Elba. I thought he was mean and sulky, but as I didn't see him between the ages of eleven and twenty-four, perhaps it was too early to judge."

"And when you were twenty-four, he came back and fell in love with you. Is that it?"

"You're a bad observer and a worse guesser and you don't listen. I've told you: we loathed one another."

"You're sure of that?"

"I could prove it. Would you mind going away?"

"Do you want to cry again?"

"Yes, I do. But I'd rather do it alone."

He left me, and I cried and cried. It didn't make me feel any better. It made me feel much worse.

Chapter Seven

I stayed in bed for a day, and on the following morning paid my routine visit to Madame in her room. Her bed was littered with even more papers than usual; snatching at them, she shuffled them into some kind of order and handed them to me with the information that the time-table for the journey to Scotland was now complete; please to type it.

I glanced at it. Apparently a convoy of three cars was to set off from London—Madame's, James's, Eden's—proceed by way of the Welsh mountains and the English lakes, and approach Edinburgh via the Western Highlands. I told her that I would take it downstairs and let James examine it.

He was having his breakfast. When I came in, he got up and addressed me with exaggerated solicitude.

"Are you quite better? Are you sure you should be up? Has the doctor given his permission for you to resume work? How do you feel after your accident, if it was an accident?" Ignoring this, I ordered my coffee and pulled it up on the hatch. I drank it sitting opposite to him, watching him turning Madame's closely written sheets. He put them down at last and slid them across the table to me.

119

"All we need is a courier," he commented. "Tell Madame it's a picturesque route, but if she's taking it, she ought to set off right away."

"You tell her," I said.

"Did you lose your courage in that fall?"

"The arrangements for this journey are nothing to do with me. It's a matter between you and Madame."

"How did three cars get into the act?" he demanded. "I've seen much too much of Croft and Patterson already. They're your friends, not mine. Tell them we'd rather make this journey without them."

"I didn't invite them."

"I didn't say you did. All you did was allow Madame to drift into making a party of it."

''Madame doesn't drift. She's equipped with a pretty powerful engine."

"Well, there's going to be no convoy. I'll fix a route and we can all meet at a specified hotel at night. We're putting on a play, not a circus." He paused and felt in his pockets. "Damn—I wrote out a paper I wanted you to type for me. I've left it upstairs; I'll go and get it." He turned from the door and surveyed me with almost genuine concern. "Incidentally, do you feel up to working?"

"Incidentally, yes."

He gave his slow smile and closed the door. When it opened again a few moments later, I didn't even bother to turn round—but it wasn't James. It was Eden.

He halted in the doorway.

"Oh, I'm sorry. I thought Maitland was in here."

"He went upstairs to fetch something. He'll be down in a moment."

James's breakfast tray was still on the table. His plate was scraped clean, as usual, but there was still toast and marmalade, untouched, and coffee in his cup. It would have looked absurd for Eden to suggest waiting for him in the study, though he was obviously longing to do just that.

"Sit down," I invited. "Would you like some coffee?"

"No, thank you."

There was a pause. I knew he felt trapped. It was the first time we had been alone since our conversation in the study. His manner was distant but polite, but I was under no illusion as to what I had seen on his face when he had made the mistake of coming into the study without knocking and had seen me in Neil's arms.

The moments went by and James didn't reappear, and presently Eden got up and walked to the window and looked out.

"Nice day," he said.

"For the time of year."

He turned and stood with his back to the window.

"Should you be up so soon after that fall you had?" he inquired.

121

"I didn't break any bones."

"How about shock?"

"I feel all right, thank you."

I remembered, fleetingly, the surprise I had felt at my god-mother's steady refusal to be charmed; he had all the equipment that the older generation usually found so reassuring: good manners, an air quiet to gentleness, an outstanding talent for saying the right thing at the right time. But she had from the first shown little liking for him. Now, I could see why—then, I had been amazed and hurt and resentful.

I finished my coffee and rose.

"Where's Margaret?" I asked.

"She said she'd be along later to see how you were."

"Good."

He opened the door for me; as I went out, I saw James Maitland advancing from the hall.

"Hello, Croft," he said. I was walking past him and he seized my arm. "Don't go yet, Alison. As Croft's here, we may as well discuss this trek to the north."

He drew me into the dining-room and closed the door.

"Those papers that Alison's holding," he told Eden, "are the time-table Madame's just drawn up for the journey to Scotland. If we were all going tiger-shooting in Assam, it couldn't be more elaborate. I can deal with that, but what I feel is that three cars are going to make the journey a bit cumbersome. How do you feel about it?"

"You'd like us to go up on our own?" Eden inquired.

"I don't see why you shouldn't. Do you really want to undergo a series of picnics on the road with Madame?"

"Since you ask me, I'd rather enjoy it," said Eden. "But I'm not really the person you should talk to; you should ask Neil and Margaret. As a matter of fact, I understood from Margaret that she'd already agreed with Alison that we should go up in convoy."

"Well, I don't want to spoil anybody's fun," James said, "but if all you see on the journey is my tail light, don't say I'm being unsociable. Which reminds me; did you drop in to see me, or to see Alison?"

"He came to see you," I said, "and if you'll give me that letter you're holding, I'll go away and leave you together."

I had just finished typing the sheet when he strolled into the study. I handed him the work I had done.

"Do you want to check it?" I asked.

"Why check it? You never make a mistake. Even Croft can't put you out of your stride. I suppose you wouldn't care to tell me the full story?"

"What story?"

"It begins: Once upon a time there were three Scots and an Outsider. I wish I could say that the ending was the usual they-lived-happily-ever-after, but I can't really say that it looks like that to me."

"I liked you the way you were before," I said. "Uninterested."

"Watching the four of you is like watching a quartet of cats squaring up for an encounter."

"Still wrong," I said. "The tactics, such as they are, are evasive."

"That's what I thought—at first. But what's so evasive about accepting invitations to this house, as they all do? What's so evasive about forming a wagon train for a slow trip to Scotland? If you won't tell me the story, all I've got to go on is my faulty observation, and even that might have led me astray yesterday, because when you fell over the banisters, what I observed in three pairs of eyes was the fear of God. Madame looked frightened enough, but your three friends looked as though death had walked in at the door."

"When you're through with your uncle's tragedy," I advised, "sit down and write a nice chilly mystery."

He gazed at me thoughtfully for a moment or two.

"You haven't been out with Neil again. Why not?"

"Because I don't want to."

"Have you quarrelled?"

"No."

"But you had some sort of showdown with Croft, didn't you?"

"Some sort of."

"Apart from Patterson, you don't seem to go out much. Why is that?"

124

"I go out whenever I want to."

"I didn't mean driving Madame around to dressmakers, and I didn't mean running errands. Don't you ever go out on your own—to theatres, to dances? When I say on your own, naturally I mean with a male escort."

"I don't know many people in London."

"Have you lived for nearly two years with Madame without meeting young people, without going out with young people, without getting together with young people?"

"I was with young people all the time I was in Scotland."

"How old are you?"

"Twenty-six."

"Weren't you afraid of burying yourself like this?"

"Weren't you telling me only the other day that I had London at my door ?—There's the doorbell. Are you expecting anybody?"

"No."

He went to the door and a moment later I heard Neil Patterson's voice. They came back together to the study.

"I could have rung you up," Neil was saying, "but I thought I'd come along. Young Hume's down with measles."

David Hume was nineteen, the youngest member of the cast, but we all felt strongly that he was too old to catch measles.

"Now what?" James asked.

"He wants his younger brother to be tried for the part. I

125

thought we could go along now and look at him."

"All right. Wait for me; I'll bring the car round," James said.

When he had gone, Neil turned to me.

"Oughtn't you to be resting?" he inquired.

His tone was quiet, even solicitous, but his face had its old habitual brooding look.

"I'm all right," I said.

"Are you sure?"

"Quite sure."

"It was a fool thing to do."

"I know. I can feel it in my bones."

"Would you come out to dinner tonight?"

"I don't think so, thank you."

"Going with someone else?"

"No."

"Then—?"

"All we agreed on was a truce."

"And I kissed you—is that it?'

"By and large." I looked at his dark, moody face. "At this moment, it's hard to imagine you kissing anybody."

"Eden saw me kissing you—and didn't like it. But Maitland was wrong about those—what did he call them?"

"Manifestations of temperament."

"There haven't been any. Eden's been more co-operative,

from that moment, than I've ever known him. That seems to me a good reason for kissing you again."

I said that I didn't agree with him, and was glad to hear James hooting impatiently. Neil hesitated and then turned and walked out of the room.

A little while later, Madame came in, but I wasn't able to tell her what James had thought of her time-table. James told her at lunch in two impolite sentences, and offered her a terse choice: she and I could travel according to the timetable, or we could join him on the rather more direct route through Oxford, York and Carlisle.

For the first time, they quarrelled. When I say they quarrelled, I mean that Madame did the quarrelling while James sat listening with polite interest. When she had given him a summary in English and Norwegian of what she thought of him, he repeated exactly what he had said in the first place.

Over coffee in the drawing-room, Madame—without a single reference to the time-table or to James's character or to the quarrel—suddenly said that she had a new idea: to go by way of Oxford, York and Carlisle. It occurred to me that I could learn much from her habit of behaving as if what happened had never happened at all.

"Oxford the first night, York the second night, and Carlisle the third night. That ought to satisfy your craze for lingering by the wayside. I haven't decided on hotels yet," James said, "but that can wait until later. We'll meet for breakfast and for dinner on the journey and the time in between will be our own."

"For myself, I shall picnic each day," said Madame.

"For myself," said James, "I detest flies, I'm frightened of cows and I never sit on wet grass."

"You are so stupid," Madame said, but her voice was indulgent. "I will give in to you because I enjoyed myself last night. The dinner was excellent and the play... well, you could not help the play."

"I enjoyed it," James said, "I thought of taking Alison to see it."

For just a moment Madame was unable to conceal her surprise. Then she rallied.

"That is a good idea," she said. "Why not take her tonight?"

James strolled slowly towards the door.

"There's no hurry," he said.

Chapter Eight

Madame, having fallen in with James's plan to travel north by way of Oxford, York and Carlisle, waited for him to draw up a detailed time-table, but all he said, and continued to say, was that when the day came, we would set off.

I imagined he had chosen the somewhat roundabout route for its historical or scenic interest, but I learned that we were going to Oxford because he wanted to look over his old college; to York because he wanted to look up a Norwegian girl who was working there, and to Carlisle because a friend of his had inherited a castle nearby and had invited him to drop in at any time and to bring his friends. If we were making a trip of it, he observed, it was only sense to look up old friends, and would I please stop Madame from badgering him about exact dates and exact times? Who could fix definite times on a trip of this kind? Anything from a puncture to a major accident would shoot time-schedules to pieces. I could tell Madame, if her blood pressure rose too high, that we would be leaving on the Thursday and not the Friday, because Christine thought Friday departures unlucky.

Getting Madame's financial, professional and personal

affairs into order before the journey soon required all my attention; as always, she confined herself to making unworkable suggestions and issuing contradictory orders. I knew by now that all I had to do was to agree to all she said, and go on doing whatever had to be done—which was practically everything.

Nobody who saw her stepping into her car on the day of departure, dressed in a voluminous travelling-cloak of Hunting Stewart tartan, her hair springing out on all sides of a glengarry with a ribbon fluttering behind, could have realised what a triumph of organisation I had achieved. Only the cook and the daily women knew—and perhaps James Maitland was beginning to guess. Her suitcases and mine were strapped on to the luggage-grid. The tape-recorder, the camera and dress-suit and the umbrella that James had at the last moment taken out of his car for fear of incommoding his passengers and left lying in the hall, were placed at Madame's feet.

I made Madame comfortable at the back of the car and walked round and took my place at the wheel. I had reached the corner of the road when a wild hooting sounded behind us. A moment later, James's car drew alongside.

"Half a moment!" he shouted.

I drew the car to the side of the road and he came round to address me irritably through my window.

"Look, I can't fit half Christina's stuff into my car. You'll have to take the rest."

Madame leaned forward.

"How much is this rest?" she inquired angrily. "I am not a pantechnicon. If you cannot fit in everything, it must be left behind."

"How much is there?" I asked him.

"There's a damn great case the size of a cabin trunk, for a start."

"Cabin trunk?" screamed Madame. "Shall I destroy my springs with cabin trunks? Alison, drive on."

I glanced ahead at James's car, which was parked in front of Madame's. The hood was down, the sun shone on the blue cushions. Christina was sitting sideways, her head turned to watch us; her expression was one of fury.

"When you ask a girl to be a passenger in the car the size of mine, do you expect," demanded James of Madame, "that she'd expect me to hook a trailer on the back for her luggage?"

"Of course I expect!" shouted Madame. "Of course anybody would expect! Anybody but you. The girl is an actress, the girl is also a harlot, the girl has valuable possessions. Did you expect that an actress about to play an important leading part would travel with simply a knapsack? If you thought sometimes of somebody but yourself, you would understand more about these things. But all you thought of was to take a girl with you to amuse you when there was no scenery. Alison, drive on. All this too-much-luggage is nothing to do with me."

I put the car into gear. James leaned over and seized the wheel.

131

"Wait a minute," he said, "and try to make Madame use her head for once. I've got to get Christina up to Edinburgh and I've got to get her luggage up there too. You can see how pleased she is with my suggestion of repacking one or two of her cases and leaving one or two things behind. If you'll drive to a garage, we can have a luggage-grid fixed on to the roof of this car."

"No luggage-grid!" yelled Madame. "I have one at the back. Finish!"

By way of answer, James opened my door.

"Get out," he said to me. "I'll drive Madame; you can drive Christine. Take her down to that garage on the next corner; there's a cafe next door, and you can fill her up with hot coffee until I get this thing sorted out."

I walked over to the other car and took the wheel.

"Well?" Christina inquired. "What is that fool going to do?"

"James is going to have a luggage-grid put on top of Madame's car."

"Ah, so that is why Madame is shouting?"

"Yes. I'm going to take you somewhere for coffee while we're waiting."

She settled back in her seat.

"Can you imagine?" she said. "He comes to my hotel and says 'Your suitcase is ready?' Suitcase! He is crazy, crazy, crazy. I wish that I had gone with Oskar."

Oskar caught us up at Oxford, clearing my mind of any doubts I might have had as to why Christina had left me in the cafe in order to make a lengthy telephone call. Perhaps she regretted having made it, for although Oskar's car was longer and faster and more beautiful than James's, Oskar himself was very much shorter than James and was frankly ugly. About their respective speeds I couldn't speak.

"I will go sometimes with one, and sometimes with the other," Christina announced to the two scowling owners.

I could see her dilemma. It wasn't only the car; it was also the wrist-watch, surrounded by so many diamonds that I wondered how she could see the time. It was the heavy gold bracelet from which dangled more than a dozen solid gold charms. All this and more, she had confided to me in the cafe, Oskar had given her.

We were not a happy party, nor even a comfortable one. In his eagerness to look over his old college at Oxford, James had omitted to book rooms at a hotel and no accommodation was available. It was about half-past six; the evening promised to be as lovely as the day had been, but nobody was in a mood to appreciate the weather. We sat outside the hotel on a small strip of lawn and had drinks and waited for Neil and Eden and Margaret to arrive. When they came, at about seven, it was Madame who informed them that owing to her nephew's thoughtfulness and foresight they were all to spend the night in a field.

"Have you rung up any other hotels?" Neil asked James.

"Of course I have. I've spent a fortune at that phone. Nothing." James answered.

Neil looked thoughtful for a while.

"I know a place," he said at last. "I don't know whether it would be full or not. It's not in the luxury class."

"Do you mean the Eagle?" Eden asked.

"Yes. Remember it?"

Eden remembered it.

"That's a good idea," he said. "Want me to ring up?"

"No, I'll do it."

Neil wasn't away long. When he came back, he addressed Madame.

"I've found accommodation," he said. "It's a plain sort of hotel, but I don't think you'll be too uncomfortable. It's run by friends of mine."

"It will be better than a field," said Madame. "At this time of year, not to book is madness."

This was true. Even Oskar had been unable to find suitable accommodation for himself or for Christina or for both.

"Perhaps I, too, can find room at your friends' hotel?" he suggested.

"You can come and try," Neil said.

Eden drove away first, Margaret beside him. She went without a backward glance. She had sat beside me on the hotel lawn without uttering more than six words. If these were Eden's wishes, I felt that she was indulging them rather too far.

134

Neil joined Madame at the back of her car. It seemed a long way to the Eagle Hotel. I rarely saw Eden's car, which was in the lead; I sometimes glimpsed James's. He had put the hood up, which was perhaps the reason why Oskar drove so close behind. I followed Oskar, who looked so lonely that when he halted for petrol, Neil asked me to draw up beside him, and ask him to take Madame as a passenger in his car. Thereafter I drove alone with Neil, which was better than having to listen to Madame's complaints. I could not help feeling sorry for her, because the business of accommodating Christina's luggage had delayed us until it was almost time for lunch; the luggage-grid once fixed on the car, James and Christina had left us and vanished into the distance, leaving Madame and myself to a picnic lunch in a setting far from sylvan. I knew that she was tired and apprehensive about the arrangements for the night.

The driving pace, always fast, had quickened. Sometimes I caught a glimpse of signposts, but mostly I didn't. We were in open and rather picturesque country, but as the light faded, a slight haze drew my attention from the passing scene and made me concentrate on keeping Oskar's car in view.

I went round a curve of road to see that the cars ahead of me had halted. I drew up behind them on a narrow country lane that branched off the main road. On the corner was a garage named Thomas's; Neil got out and joined Eden in a friendly reunion with the proprietor, Mr. Thomas. I began to edge the car towards one of the pumps, but Neil called to me.

"Not now," he said. "You can get petrol tomorrow morning. The hotel's just up the hill."

He pointed skywards and we all craned our necks to look.

It was certainly a hill. The lane, after a few level yards, rose so steeply that I wondered if I could get Madame's heavily-laden car up it—but there wasn't much time to wonder. Neil had seated himself once more beside me, and one by one the cars went at the ascent like horses going at a jump. It seemed to me unusual to be going straight up the side of a hill rather than taking the more normal way round it; Neil explained that this method had saved the Thomases a good deal of money— road-making money.

We drove on, up and up—and then, with startling suddenness, the road levelled. About a hundred yards ahead we saw the hotel rightly called the Eagle.

It was a homely-looking place. Eden told us its history. Mr. Thomas, who owned the garage on the road below, and whom we had seen as he spoke to Neil and Eden, had married a retired theatrical dresser named Jenny. It was Jenny who, gazing upwards from the garage, had conceived the idea of building a small hotel at the top. It was built and named the Eagle. Later, to supply fresh produce for its guests, Jenny and her stalwart son Tom had cultivated the flat shelf of land half way down the hill, and on it built a small cottage. Today, the garage was old Tom's concern, the hotel Jenny's and the farm young Tom's.

Jenny led us all inside while young Tom undertook the

tricky task of turning all the cars on the limited space avail-able and leaving them facing the road. I took a last look at the gradient and decided that tomorrow I would ask Oskar to take Madame down in his car.

Once inside the hotel, I rather regretted that we were only to spend one night there, for I felt strangely at home. The place seemed to me to have the squareness and simplicity and clean-liness of houses I had seen in Scotland, while Jenny and her husband, with their forthright speech and calm good sense, could have been typical Scots.

Madame was talking to James in Norwegian and seemed to be repeating what she had said earlier in English about his organising abilities. Oskar was talking to Christina in German, saying—I imagined—that if matters had been in his hands, he wouldn't have put a girl like her in a place like this. Marga-ret had gone up to her room. Neil and Eden were exchanging reminiscences with Jenny about past theatrical occasions. The only other guests—a somewhat self-conscious honeymoon couple, whom Jenny introduced by telling us that they were both related to her on her Uncle Bernard's side—sat in the small bar and stared out at us with interest.

Dinner did a great deal to restore the spirits of Madame and Oskar. It was a plain meal, but it was well cooked and there was plenty of it. Dishes were placed down the middle of the table, and when I saw what they contained, I wondered how we could get through so much food—but there was noth-ing left in them when Jenny cleared them away. The pea soup, the roast beef and Yorkshire pudding, the roast potatoes, the cabbage, the three great apple tarts and the two pitchers of cream all disappeared; the more we ate, the happier Jenny became.

She had not been in the theatre for nothing; she could do a little acting herself and she understood temperament; both Madame and Christina, therefore, went up to bed happy in the knowledge that they had each been given the best room in the house. My own room was over the kitchen, which made it warm but noisy; I fell asleep to the sound of Jenny and the two Toms and the honeymoon couple at their supper.

I slept dreamlessly and woke early. I went to the window and looked out at a wide view of countryside partly obscured by rain. I made my way to the only bathroom, found it unoccupied, had a swift bath and went back to my room to dress and pack. I carried my suitcase downstairs and met Jenny in the hall.

"You're early, love," she said. "Didn't you sleep?"

"I slept beautifully, thank you. I rather like getting up early."

"So do I," Jenny said. "Do you want to wait and have breakfast with the others, or will you come and join Tom and his dad and me?"

"All I want is coffee," I said.

"Nonsense, love, nonsense! At your age, and with your figure? You come along and get a good meal inside you before you start off with that sour old bitch. Come along in."

I sat down at the kitchen table opposite young Tom, with old Tom on my right and Jenny on my left.

"The young couple aren't down," old Tom observed.

"Why should they be, on their honeymoon?" inquired Jenny. "You've got a short memory, that's what's the matter with you."

I found myself, to my amazement, working steadily through fried eggs, thick slices of bacon and succulent liver that Jenny transferred straight from a sizzling pan on to our plates. After scones and honey and two cups of coffee, I felt ready to face the day.

I went upstairs to see Madame, who said that she had slept as well as could be expected. The breakfast tray looked unfamiliar with Jenny's second best china—the best had been sent up to Christina; an actress, after all, was an actress. I was about to suggest the journey down the hill with Oskar, when Madame forestalled me.

"This morning, I am to travel with James," she said. "I wish to speak seriously with him. I think he does not understand that I am, after all, entitled to some consideration. If he thinks that I am to be swept aside in this way, he is mistaken."

"But isn't Christina—" I began.

"I am sick of this Christina. She will travel with Oskar. What she can see in James when she can have the attention of a man of the world, a charming, cultivated man like the Prince, this is what I do not understand. I said to her last night that this morning, I will take her place in James's car. This will teach him that I am not to be disregarded."

The Prince, I thought, had not wasted his time in the car with Madame. Favours were favours, and this was a big one; perhaps he would reward Madame with a gold bracelet heavy with dangling charms.

"If I'm driving alone, Madame" I said, "would you mind if I went on ahead?"

"It would be sensible to do this," she said. "Then you can go slowly. I do not like that my car is driven like a racehorse."

"Do you want me to prepare a picnic lunch?"

"Thank you, no. The Prince will arrange everything. He has a friend who has a very beautiful house on our way, and he will take me there for lunch."

"In that case, I'd better find out from James where we're staying tonight."

"James knows nothing about where we are staying to-night."

"Aren't we going to York."

"In passing, we shall see York—but we are staying for the night in a beautiful hotel that the Prince knows. It is on the moors. The Yorkshire moors. These, I told him, I had never seen. He said that he would ring up and he would arrange our hotel. If you will give me my handbag, I will tell you where it is and you can go there."

I handed her her bag and she took from it a piece of paper.

"You will drive to York, and from there you will take the road to Whitby. Do you know Whitby?"

"I've heard of it."

"Very well. You will find a signpost pointing to a place called Netherheath. When you get there, you must go to the Netherheath Inn. Can you find your way?"

I said that I could, and went downstairs with a holiday feeling. I was to be alone. I could drive as I liked, stop where I liked, picnic as I pleased. The car was mine, the day was mine and, like Madame, I had never seen the Yorkshire moors.

I went to my room, saw that nothing had been left behind, and went downstairs to say good-bye to Jenny.

"Any time you want a job, love, just you come to me," she said. "Girls like you don't need to work for old bitches."

Old Tom and young Tom helped me out with my suitcase and I said good-bye to them all with genuine regret.

"Can't I give you a lift down to the garage?" I asked old Tom, when I was settled in the car.

"That's kind of you," he said, "but I like to walk down. It's about the only real exercise I get all day."

I turned to young Tom.

"How about you?" I asked. "Can I drive you down to the farm?"

He smiled and shook his head.

"No thanks; I'll walk down," he said.

141

Jenny poked him roughly in the ribs.

"Go on with you," she said. "Do you call that polite? Here's a beautiful young lady offering you a ride, and you refuse. Go on, get in with you."

He got in, and neither he nor I knew that his mother's insistence had made all the difference to me between life and death. He got in and sat beside me and I thanked Jenny and said good-bye once more and then I released the handbrake and put the car into gear and drove away.

As I approached the end of the level road, I braked before getting the car into low gear to take the hill. But the car, instead of checking, went on—and I faced the steep descent to the road below with the appalled realisation that the brakes were not working.

I think that during those first moments, young Tom thought I was out of my mind—but fortunately for us both, he had his mother's sense and his father's solidity. He sat quite still for a few seconds and then turned his head and met my instant's glance of panic.

"Something's wrong," I managed to say.

The car was moving with terrifying speed. I had ceased to think very clearly, but somewhere deep in my mind was a prayer that I might continue calm. Desperately I considered steering towards the low hedge, in the hope that the car would stop before tearing its way through to the grassy slope of the hill and rolling us down to almost certain death. Looking at the hedge flying past, I shed all illusions; what lay ahead was death itself.

I knew with thankfulness that I was growing calmer. I wondered if at the last I should close my eyes...

And then I felt myself being pushed violently aside. Tom's hands, huge and red and horny, appeared beside mine and gripped the wheel. I had no hope that he could save us, but I pressed close to the door in order to allow him as much freedom as possible.

I felt his hard, big body against mine as we flew on for another few seconds—and then I saw the wide gap in the hedge that gave entrance to the little farm and felt the car swerving violently as Tom pulled the wheel round. The car lurched, bumped sickeningly over the rutted ground, slowed and at last stopped.

I don't know how long the silence lasted. I turned slowly to face young Tom. His face was grey. I tried to speak, found that I couldn't and then at last managed to bring out a shaky, superfluous sentence.

"Something went wrong with the brakes."

He nodded grimly. Like me, he seemed to find speech difficult.

"You all right?" he asked at last.

"Yes." I swallowed. "Tom—"

"That's all right," he said.

I looked round. I saw that he had wrenched the wheel round and brought the car across his own farmland. What I had thought to be a ploughed field was, or had been, a neatly-kept area of flourishing green peas. The produce for the Eagle Hotel had suffered a good deal of damage—but young Tom and I were alive.

My knees were shaking. I saw young Tom pass a hand slowly across his eyes; perhaps he was wiping off that glimpse of death. Then the sound of a car turned us both towards the entrance to the farm. It was Neil driving Eden's car. Beside him sat old Tom, and we did not need to be told that they had seen us as we hurtled down the hill.

Before Neil had brought the car to a stop, old Tom was out and beside us.

"What happened, for God's sake?" he asked.

"The brakes," said young Tom. "I was just going to take a look at them."

I must have looked rather dazed, for Neil came up and, taking my arm, gave me a slight shake.

"Everything's all right," he said.

"I know."

"Has this ever happened before?" he asked.

"No, never."

"Who else saw us?" young Tom inquired. "Not—"

"Not your mother, no," his father reassured him. "When you and Miss Sinclair drove off, she went into the house. I was following her when Mr. Patterson came out, and we stood talking for a moment. I was facing the house, but he was looking at the hill; when I saw his expression change, I turned ..."

Neil led me to Eden's car.

"Get in," he ordered. "I'll drive you up to the hotel."

"No."

I spoke almost violently, and the three men looked at one another.

"Take her down to the garage," ordered old Tom. "There's a young boy down there—tell him to make her a hot cup of tea. Then if you'll come up here again, we'll do something about getting this car to rights."

Neil and I drove in silence to the garage. He stopped at the top of the lane and got out and walked across the yard to speak to a boy of about fifteen; then he came back to me.

"You'll get tea," he said, "but it might take some time; it depends on the number of cars that stop for petrol. There's only one fellow on duty until old Tom comes down."

I got out and sat on a wooden bench and watched the car as it turned and went up the hill to the farm. The lane was quiet and leafy, but just round the corner was the main road with its busy traffic. I sat watching the cars streaming by and wondered if I would ever again feel a sense of security when driving. Sound brakes were something I had always taken for granted; if one wanted to stop, there was a pedal or there was a lever; one used one or the other and the car came obediently to a halt. Now I had a sense of betrayal; my whole conception of cars had undergone a radical change. I had hitherto been concerned only with getting them started; now I had a sickening realisation of the importance of getting them stopped.

I got up and walked into the garage, and in a dingy little office came upon a gas stove on which was a steaming kettle. I emptied cold tea leaves out of a tea pot and made fresh tea; I rinsed two dirty cups under a tap and took out the bottle of milk that protruded from the saddle bag of the boy's bicycle. When he had filled up the car standing outside, cleaned its windscreen and sent it on its way, I called to him.

"Tea's ready."

He came in, wiping his hands on an oily rag.

"I don't want any sugar," I told him, "but if you do, I can't find it."

Grinning, he reached over and produced from a shelf a tobacco tin full of sugar.

"I've gorra coupla buns if you'd like 'em," he offered.

"No, thank you. You eat them."

We sat in the fume-laden garage drinking our tea, and I watched his irregular, not-too-clean teeth biting into the buns and wished very much that we could go on sitting there indefinitely, drinking tea and talking about the latest television comedians.

A car drove up and stopped and the boy put down his cup, wiped his mouth, and went out to the petrol pump. I was left to look at two second-hand cars painted to look like new and labelled For Sale, a derelict motorbike and, in the dim background, two cars of antique design with their bonnets yawning wide like hungry monsters.

The tea had made me feel a little better. I got up and walked out into the narrow lane and saw Eden's car coming down the hill. It stopped beside me and Neil got out.

"We fixed the brakes," he said. "Old Tom's bringing the car down—but you're not going to drive it today. I am."

I had nothing to say against this; I thought it an admirable arrangement. I had a craven plan in my mind: to keep my hand on the handle of the door on my side, ready to leap out next time the car bolted.

"I'm going up to the hotel to leave Eden's car there," Neil said. "Tom's driving Madame's car down to the garage because he wants to do some more work on it. I'll walk down from the hotel."

"Don't tell them," I said.

"Why not?"

His tone told me that he had said "Why don't you want me to?" rather than "Why shouldn't they know?"

"Two accidents in three weeks are two too many," I explained. "First I dive over the banisters—and now this. People will begin to think it's exhibitionism. Did anybody else see the car coming down the hill?"

"Not as far as I know. There was no sign of anybody around. I heard Maitland in the bathroom and I think the others were still in bed."

147

We turned to watch Madame's car, driven by old Tom, coming slowly down the hill. Young Tom was seated beside his father. They went past us into the garage, and then the two men got out.

"How're you feeling?" old Tom asked.

"I'm all right, thanks. I suppose you know that Tom saved my life."

"And his own. He's a brave fellow when it comes to saving his own life," old Tom said. "Do you do all the driving for Madame?"

"Yes."

"Cars need check-ups sometimes; did you ever think of that."

"I have it regularly serviced."

"You mean you leave it at the garage and hope they do all they should. Well, sometimes they do and sometimes they don't.—Now, if you'll sit on that bench over there and rest yourself, we'll get these brakes fixed properly and put our signature on the job—which means that you won't need to have any fear in the future. Why don't you drive up with Mr. Patterson to the hotel till we're ready for you?"

"I'd rather stay here, if you don't mind," I said.

I didn't stay there. I crossed the main road and took a path through the woods that lay on the other side. It was a brilliant morning and I remembered that it was a long time since I had walked in woods. It was a long time since I had seen the sun

148

filtering through leaves and setting a gently- quivering carpet at my feet.

A wave of homesickness rose and almost engulfed me. I saw, as clearly as though I had been standing before it, the big square stone house with its backing of splendid old trees, its terraced gardens, its neat paths, its curving drive. I could see my godmother clearly—now coming down the steps of the house, upright, neatly dressed, neatly gloved, to get into her small neat car and drive away to Edinburgh. Now she was walking round the garden with old Angus, arguing about the possible connection between the phases of the moon and the times of planting. She was in the kitchen helping Beatrice with the baking, or upstairs with Jinty, counting linen. She was in the drawing-room receiving the Laird or the minister or deaf old Mrs. Muir, to whom few people besides herself had patience enough to be kind. She was in my bedroom sitting on the end of my bed and suggesting gently, hopelessly, that per-haps it would be better to know something more about a man before giving my heart. She was in the hall saying good-bye to me and her voice was quiet, but when I remembered the look in her eyes, I had to close my own.

I had gone away promising to write, and I had written to her twice and I had posted the letters myself—but she had not replied ...

I don't know how long I stood there leaning against the tree. I was brought back to the present by the sight of Neil striding along the path towards me.

"I've been sounding the horn," he called. "Didn't you hear?"

"No."

He came up and looked closely at me.

"Anything the matter besides faulty brakes?" he asked.

"No, nothing."

"Then take that look off your face. I haven't seen you look like that since—"

He stopped abruptly. His black eyes stared into mine for some moments, and then he took my arm and turned me to face the path. We walked back together in silence, halting at the edge of the wood to await an opportunity to cross the main road, on which traffic was now fast and heavy in both directions. Then he opened the door of Madame's car.

"Get in and relax," he said. "I'm driving today and the brakes are working."

I was handed in by old Tom. I said a totally inadequate farewell to him and to his son.

"It's no use trying to thank you," I said.

"That's right," old Tom agreed. "It's no use, so don't try. All you've got to do is to take care of yourself, or get some nice young fellow to do it for you. It's a wonder to me you haven't done it long since. And if you want to be nice and quiet and comfortable on your honeymoon, you know where to come."

There were tears in my eyes; perhaps they expressed more than words could have done. I waved until the garage was out of sight, and then I leaned back and hoped that we could get through the day without meeting any other members of our party. But it was no longer early, and I knew that they would soon be on our heels, or on our tail light. I gave up all hope when I saw Neil turn off the road and stop at a roadhouse.

"If you remember," he said, parking the car and switching off the engine, "you had breakfast, but I didn't. D'you mind coming in and watching me while I get through some bacon and eggs?"

We were given a table on a small, sunny terrace; I drank coffee and watched Neil breakfasting as every morning I had become accustomed to watching James. Neil ate far more slowly and didn't talk with his mouth full. He also ate a good deal less.

"What do you want to do about lunch?" he asked me, when he had finished. "If you want to picnic, I could ask them to put up some food for us. It looks a pretty good day; why not eat out of doors?"

"All right" I agreed, "but I'd rather buy the food myself. The next town we go through might have one of those shops with chickens cooking on a grid."

We bought two newly-cooked chickens, bread and cheese and salad. Being unable to agree about drink, we bought wine, beer and cider, and when we drove on again, I was relieved to find that the near-tragedy of the morning was no longer in the forefront of my mind.

"I know a good place for a picnic," he said, as we drove

on. "A bit hilly, if that won't make you nervous, but with good views. It's nice and quiet. There are two quiet spots there, as a matter of fact."

So there had been, he explained later, when we reached the first spot and found that a Motel had been built upon it. So there had been, he explained later still when we had reached the second spot, to find it occupied by—so their large, bright green coach informed us—the Mintybridge and District Brass Band.

"Well, I know one place they can't ruin," Neil said in disgust. "Eden and I discovered it about twelve yeas ago; we must have been the first people who ever risked taking a car up to it."

It was certainly a hazardous drive. The road was narrow and rocky and full of potholes, but the view was lovely and grew lovelier at each bend of the track.

"Round this corner," Neil said, "there's a nice quiet grassy ledge."

On the nice quiet grassy ledge, set in a circle like pioneers' wagons fighting off Indians, were four cars: Eden's, James's, Oskar's, and a magnificent one which I had never seen before. Seated at a picnic table, waited on by a chauffeur in dark blue uniform, were Madame and Oskar, James and Christina, Eden and Margaret and an extremely stout, extremely dark, middle-aged gentleman who might have been Oskar's elder brother.

Neil, muttering curses under his breath, looked as though

152

he was about to swing the car round and drive away again, but I had already decided to stay; it was nearly two o'clock and I was ravenously hungry and the chicken they were eating looked far better than ours and was flanked by pale pink slices of ham. There was also tongue and—I thought and hoped— cold turkey. To clinch matters, they were drinking champagne from delicate misted glasses. So when the men had struggled to their feet and Oskar had presented his cousin, Mr. Bernstein, I pulled out all the stops and was presently gratified, though not surprised, to find myself seated on Mr. Bernstein's right hand with the chauffeur in close attendance.

The others were not so happy. Christina, after her morning's drive with Oskar, looked sulky and bored. Madame looked annoyed; I knew that, much as she enjoyed picnics, she had expected to eat her lunch in the comfortable dining-room of some large mansion. James looked sleepy. Eden and Margaret had a tense look, as though they had been arguing all the morning and were preparing fresh arguments for the afternoon.

I don't think I ever enjoyed a meal more. With the turkey and the chicken and the ham and the tongue I seemed to be swallowing the remains of the morning's terror. The champagne washed my mind clean of all but the sunny present. Even the sounds of soloists from the Mintybridge Brass Band, wafted to us on the warm breeze, could not disturb my mood of contentment.

By the time I had got through two helpings of chocolate

mousse, a strawberry ice and Turkish coffee, I found that I had promised Mr. Bernstein to lunch, dine and sup with him throughout the Festival. I recalled, hazily, previous unsuccessful attacks upon my virtue and wondered what would have happened if I had been offered chicken and champagne at once, instead of a trip to Paris at the week-end.

There were several attempts after lunch to bring about a change in the driving arrangements, but they came to nothing. Madame, having failed to persuade Mr. Bernstein to drive up then and there to Edinburgh with her as passenger, fell back upon James. Oskar and Christina were to be together once more; nobody suggested separating Eden and Margaret, and Neil made it clear that he would go on driving Madame's car.

I felt an overpowering urge to curl up on the grassy bank nearby and fall into a deep sleep. With the idea of fighting off drowsiness, I got to my feet and wandered away from the others; Mr. Bernstein started after me, but halted at the realisation that I might be in search of a friendly bush. I took a steep path to the left and the trees closed above my head, giving a pleasant sense of coolness. I felt ashamed of having eaten so much, and quickened my pace to work off some of the effects of lunch. The path went on, but halfway up the hill, I had seen through the thick bushes a sunny, level patch of ground. Getting to it meant breaking my way through clinging branches and sharp thorns, but when I got through at last, I felt that it had been worth it, for I found myself standing on a narrow ledge, looking down at a scene almost wild, with little streams washing over boulders, low, heather- clad hills rolling away into the distance and, immediately below the shelf on which I was standing, an almost dry, rocky river bed.

When I could take my eyes off the view and look about me, I realised that this place, which I had reached the hard way, had in fact an approach from above—a precarious arrangement of large flat stones placed so as to form rough steps up to the top of the hill. As I was gazing upwards, I heard a sound; I swung round, startled, to find to my astonishment that I was not alone. Seated with his legs dangling over the dizzy drop was a shrivelled old man dressed in the ugly, bright green uniform which I recognised as that worn by the members of the Mintybridge Brass Band. Instead of an instrument, however, he was holding a bottle; as I looked, he put it to his lips, emptied it, wiped his mouth with the back of his hand and gave me a sideways, leering look.

"Whisky," he said, in the thick, slurred accents of the very drunk. "Whisky. The best drink in the world. But not for young ladies."

"No," I agreed, and stood undecided whether to go back the way I had come, or by the steps.

"You going?" inquired the old man.

"Yes."

"You won't tell them, will you?"

"No."

I looked down at him. They were the words I had spoken

155

that morning to Neil.

"No," I said "I won't tell them."

"They make too much fuss," he explained, between hic-coughs. "Much too much fuss. They and their drotted old Band. One day I'll drown them all, so I will, but not—" he gave me a look repulsive in its slyness—"not in whisky."

I felt my first feelings of pity evaporating; he was drunk and dirty and evil-looking. I glanced at the steps and decided against them; I would go back the way I had come.

I left him peering into the bottle to discover whether it was really empty. I found it even more difficult to get out than it had been to get in, but I managed it at last and turned down-hill to rejoin the rest of the party. When I got back to the cars, however, I found only the chauffeur there. The others, he told me, had left shortly after I did, having decided to go for a walk.

I gathered up the things that Madame had left lying about—a scarf, a fountain pen, her glengarry. I put them into James's car, got into her own, curled myself up comfortably and dozed. When I opened my eyes again, it was to see stout Mr. Bernstein standing regarding me with open admiration. He was about to transfer it from his eyes to his tongue when we heard the others returning.

"I look forward to Edinburgh," was all he had time to say. Then Madame's voice reached me before she came into view. She sounded extremely agitated.

"Alison, Alison, are you there? Where are you?"

I got out of the car.

"I'm here, Madame" I said.

She came hurrying into sight and I saw that something had upset her badly. Her cheeks beneath the rouge were chalk-white and she was breathing fast.

"I am not well," she said, "I have had a bad shock."

I looked at Margaret, who was just behind her; to my astonishment, I saw that she looked even whiter than Madame. Her lips were trembling; her eyes, resting on me, were filled with horror.

The others had come into sight and I saw that all of them looked shaken. It was Oskar who volunteered an explanation.

"It is very unfortunate," he said. "There was an accident."

My eyes ran swiftly over the group; all present, all safe.

"Who?" I asked, and hoped that it had not been a child.

James answered my question.

"One of the Band," he said. "Not one of the actual performers, I gathered from what the surviving members told us. He was an old man they take around because he can still fill in if somebody falls out. He wandered away and took a bottle of whisky with him and fell down the hill on to some rocks. They found the bottle where he'd left it—empty—which makes it pretty certain that he tried to walk along a path that wasn't there. Poor devil."

"Whereabouts?" I asked. But I knew without being told.

"Apparently he fell from just above here," James said. "It

was a lethal drop down to a pile of boulders. As ends go, I suppose it was a merciful one."

I stood still. *The best drink in the world.* Perhaps he would have agreed with James—that as ends went, it was not a bad end.

"And now," Mr. Bernstein said briskly, his eyes on my face, "we will if you please forget all about accidents—which will happen whatever we can do to prevent them. I would suggest that we all drive away and meet at the hotel in Netherheath. I myself know the owners, and I shall go on ahead and see that a good reception is prepared for you all."

I looked at Margaret. She was walking slowly towards Eden's car. Neil spoke at my shoulder.

"You can't do anything," he said. "She'll get over it."

Madame appeared to have recovered; she was already in James's car, urging him to drive on. I followed Neil to her car, and he took the wheel. We didn't speak until we were back again on the open road.

"Perhaps I should have stayed with Margaret," I said. "She looked ill."

"What good could you have done?"

His mood, I saw, had not changed; he was as he had been all the morning—irritable and withdrawn. I sensed that he did not want to talk, but I wanted to hear more about the accident.

"What exactly happened?" I asked. "To the old man, I mean."

"How do I know what happened? I wasn't with the poor old devil. All I can tell you is that when you wandered away, the rest of us got up and separated, each to our own private concerns. We met again at the top of the hill; I looked for you, but you were nowhere around. I asked Margaret if she'd seen you, but she hadn't. Neither had any of the others. We decided that you must have gone back to the picnic spot, so we turned to come down the hill—and then had to stand aside to make room for a party of Bandsmen who were carrying up the body of the old man. It wasn't a scene you'd want to come upon in the middle of a picnic, and it isn't a scene anyone wants to dwell on or talk about, so now would you mind forgetting it?"

"I saw him," I said.

He was so startled that for an instant the car swerved. He pulled it back and brought it to an abrupt stop; the brakes were working so well that I almost went through the windscreen.

"Would you mind giving notice—" I began angrily.

"Did you say you *saw* him?"

"Yes."

"You mean you walked down those damned dangerous-looking steps?"

"No. I broke a way through the bushes halfway up the hill. I thought I was alone and then I saw the old man sitting on the edge of the ledge with his feet hanging over. He was very drunk. He was a horrible-looking old man, but that doesn't make it less awful. I wish I'd stayed a bit longer; I wish I'd stayed, at any rate, until he got to his feet; then perhaps I could have turned him round towards the steps and he wouldn't have stepped over the edge."

Neil said nothing. He started the car once more and drove on at a pace that would have brought violent protests from Madame. From that moment until we drew up outside the Netherheath Inn, he didn't speak more than a dozen words; after making two or three attempts to engage him in conversation and getting nothing but terse responses, I left him to himself.

But I enjoyed every moment of the drive. I was given no time to linger, but there was time enough to look. There was time enough to enjoy, before dusk came, the wild beauty of the moors. I had wondered if the heather would remind me of Scotland, but there was nothing Scottish in the scene; the light seemed to me clearer and harder, the hills lower and less lovely, the sea, when at last it came in sight, without the greyish-green look that I loved so much.

It was dark and rather cold when we got to the hotel. It was also rather late, so that I was hungry again; the sight of Mr. Bernstein standing with a welcoming look in the square, brightly-lit hall made me think longingly of dinner.

There were, I soon found, other angles to Mr Bernstein besides chicken and champagne; instead of being shown to the modest chamber usually allotted to Madame's secretaries, I found myself in a comfortable room which had a fire burning brightly in the grate and a bathroom all of its own. Mr. Bernstein was a kind man, I thought, and tested the lock on my door. It seemed sound enough, and I saw that the corridor outside was too narrow to allow him to take a running jump at it, even if he could manage, with his figure, to achieve a running jump. I locked the door, undressed and had a long, unhurried bath. I felt so festive after it that I thought of putting on my pale green with the plunging neck line—and then decided against it; it was no use enflaming Mr. Bernstein.

We all dined together at a long table placed near a roaring log fire down the centre of the hotel dining-room, the other guests being relegated to the dim, cold recesses of the room. It was a good meal, and by the end of it, we were all agreed that the Lubin play was going to be the Festival's chief success, the name of Lubin due for world fame and that nothing was so delightful as a drive to Edinburgh at this time of the year. Only Neil seemed apart from this lightness of spirit; seated beside Margaret, he seemed to have shaken off the dark mood of the afternoon, but he ate little, drank less and said almost nothing. I thought he looked pale, but I knew that any solicitous inquiries would receive rough treatment, and so I made none.

Mr. Bernstein had, with more ardour than tact, seated me upon his right hand; I had felt strongly that this place should be Madame's and had done my best to cede it to her, but had had to stop short of making a fuss. When dinner was over, however, Madame—from motives either protective or petulant—decided to make a bid for his attention. She cut him out of the herd with the skill of an old hunter and bore him away to a tête-à-tête in a far corner of the lounge.

I wandered into the hall, found a shelf of books, selected one and decided to go upstairs to bed. James Maitland, on his way across the hall, saw me halfway up the stairs and called to me.

"You're not going to bed so early?"

"Yes, I am."

He took the stairs in three bounds and hurried along the corridor in my wake.

"But look here, we're thinking of getting up a game of *vingt-et-un*."

"You do that," I said kindly.

"Don't you want to play?"

"No. I've got a nice fire in my room and I'm going to make the most of it. Good night."

"But you can't leave poor old Bernstein trapped all the evening with Madame!"

"He's a man of the world; Madame herself told me so. If he can't get himself out of situations like this, it's time he learnt."

I was in my room. He leaned against the doorpost and surveyed the comfortable scene.

"You look pretty well set up in here," he commented. "My room hasn't got a fire and it hasn't got a bathroom."

"Too bad," I said. "Maybe you're not Mr. Bernstein's type."

"I wouldn't have said you were, either. You keep surprising me. Look—if I brought a book, I could sit and read by the fire. I wouldn't disturb you."

"Wrong again. You would."

I began to close the door and he backed reluctantly into the corridor.

"Anyway, you've given me an idea," he said. "I'll go to bed myself. It's been a long day, and thinking about that poor chap doesn't make one feel any better."

"It was a good end. You said so yourself."

"I know I did—but that was only to calm the spirits of all present. In actual fact, it would depend on whether the poor old devil saw it coming or not."

I stared at him.

"Saw it coming?" I repeated slowly, and saw James's eyes fixed with astonishment on my own.

"How do you think he died?" he asked.

"He was drunk and he walked over the edge. You said so."

"I didn't think there was any point in going into details. Didn't Neil tell you what happened?"

"Neil didn't want to talk about it. Didn't he walk over the edge?"

"Not exactly. He was drunk, of course, but what those pall-bearers actually told us was that he happened to be standing in the path of a boulder that had got loose and crashed down the side of the hill. He went down with it, or before it, or under it, nobody'll ever know which."

I made no reply. I closed the door and locked it and turned and stood staring straight before me.

A boulder crashing down the hillside. A boulder crashing down on to the spot where I had been standing. If I had stood there a little longer, a few minutes longer, perhaps only a few seconds longer...

My mind went back to old Tom and young Tom and the hotel and the farm and the garage. I saw a hedge rushing by faster and faster and faster—and then I saw a boulder crashing down a hill. . .

I got into bed and opened the book and read for some time—and then I got out of bed again with the feeling that I ought to give thanks where thanks were due. So I knelt down and thanked God with great fervour for my lucky day.

Chapter Nine

I didn't go to sleep for a long time; when at last I did, I slept heavily and dreamlessly. I woke early—too early to hope for morning tea. I thought of dressing and going for a walk, but the mist outside and the fine, drizzling rain made me change my mind.

I picked up my book and read until my morning tea was brought in—but neither the book nor the tea could keep my mind from dwelling on the events of yesterday. Try as I would to think of other things, I found myself going back again and again to matters that I felt were better forgotten.

My godmother, I knew, could have helped me—but she was out of reach. She knew these moods of mine, when my brain refused to deal with new matters and revolved obstinately and maddeningly around affairs that I had thought over and done with; when my mind seemed bogged down in a confusion of ideas from which something seemed to be struggling to emerge. She had always been able to bring order out of the disorder; she had always put her finger on the conclusion I was attempting to reach. Without her aid, the process of enlightenment was longer and far more difficult.

By the time I was dressed, the drizzle had stopped and the sun was beginning to come out. I would have liked to miss breakfast and go for a long walk, but I had to go in and see Madame. Knocking on her door, I wondered what kind of reception I would get; she had not, I knew, enjoyed herself yesterday; as usual, she would probably work off some of her disappointment on me and as usual it would do her some good and do me no harm.

I found her, to my surprise, in the best of spirits.

"Good morning, Alison. You slept well?"

"Yes, thank you, Madame. And you?"

"Extremely well. This bed is comfortable, this place is charming and the air is magnificent. If I could afford it, I would like to have a little cottage up here."

I nodded sympathetically. Like most of the rest of us, she would have liked a cottage on the moors, a flat in town, a chalet by the sea and a cabin up in the snows.

"It was a pity you went to bed early," she told me. "You didn't hear what Mr. Bernstein has fixed for us. He is a very kind man, but he is not for girls like you. I think he is more for Christina."

Christina, I could have pointed out, had her hands full. Instead, I waited to hear what Mr. Bernstein had fixed.

"We are to have lunch with Lord and Lady Weaver. Perhaps you have not heard of them?"

I said that I had.

"They have a large house some miles—forty, I think—from here. Mr. Bernstein telephoned to them last night and we are all to go there. He says that the house and the gardens are beautiful. We shall all enjoy it."

I found myself wondering how much Margaret and Eden would enjoy it. The house had been lent to them for their honeymoon—but they did not seem to have mentioned this fact to Madame.

"We shall get there about half past twelve and be in time to have some drinks before lunch. I would have liked to stay for tea also, but when I said this, James and the others began to make a fuss. My wishes are always disregarded."

Her breakfast tray was brought in and I waited to see if she wanted anything more; then I went back to my room to pack.

When the time for departure came, I found that I had been allocated to Mr. Bernstein, perhaps as a reward for his admirable arrangements for our comfort. The journey was accomplished without incident, the presence of his chauffeur preventing Mr. Bernstein from doing more than taking my hand and enfolding it in his own warm, well-cushioned ones. He asked, somewhat wistfully, if I cared for cruising; he had a comfortably fitted yacht and September was a delightful month in the Mediterranean. I told him that my ambition was a husband and four children and summer holidays at North Berwick. After this brief exchange, he proved an intelligent and interesting travelling companion and I felt that I would have enjoyed seeing more of him—if I could have taken out the fuse.

I wasn't surprised when Eden's car flashed by us; I guessed that he and Margaret would want to get to the house before the rest of us, in order to get over, before we arrived, the inevitable references to the past. I could almost hear Eden suggesting that it would be better to say nothing of honeymoons in our presence; there was a risk, he would point out, that somebody like Madame might be led into making arch or embarrassing comments.

The car had entered an avenue lined with magnificent beech trees; on either side was an extensive deer park. The house proved to be ugly but imposing, with an outcrop of square towers and conical turrets out of tune with the lovely setting. We were given a warm welcome by our hosts, and drinks on a terrace that ran the entire length of one side of the building. No reference was made by either Lord or Lady Weaver to Eden and Margaret's previous occupation of the house.

Lunch, to Madame's satisfaction, was today served with ceremony, but there was no champagne and the chicken was lost in a stodgy mess of rice and made far too heavy a meal for so sunny a day.

The combination of heavy food and hot afternoon seemed to drain the guests of energy. Conversation flagged and died; only Lord Weaver, kind and hospitable and totally oblivious to atmosphere, droned on. His audience, bored and apathetic, dealt with a leaden sponge pudding, tasteless cheese and a long and detailed account of the way in which a poacher on the estate had at last been caught red-handed by Lord Weaver himself and handed over to justice.

We were, Neil announced authoritatively at the end of lunch, to leave at four o'clock sharp—without tea. We had coffee on the terrace, after which Lady Weaver suggested that we might all like to look at the garden.

I didn't want to look at the garden; I wanted a long, swift walk. Madame wanted to sit and enjoy the view. Neil wanted to read the morning papers and James wanted to go to sleep. None of us could voice these preferences openly, but by adroit manoeuvring we managed to get what we wanted. I took a short cut through the kitchen garden and the paddock and struck out across the park, my goal a little coppice that promised shade from the hot afternoon sun.

I reached it and sat at the foot of a tree and thought that this would be the perfect place from which to take a photograph of the house; the side of it that I could see looked plain and square and uncompromising, but it had none of the over-elaboration we had seen as we drove up. The towers and the turrets were there, but they were not too much in evidence. Beyond the house was a glimpse of rose garden and I could see some figures just going out of view: Lord Weaver, Mr. Bernstein, Eden and Margaret.

I leaned against the tree and closed my eyes. I was sitting half in sunlight, half in shadow; the silence was almost complete, broken only by the sound of birds and the distant, muted throb of a motor mower moving across the wide, smooth lawns. Behind me, sheltering me from the light breeze that had sprung up, were thick bushes and trees; in front of me was nothing but a stretch of beautiful open parkland with the house at the end. To the left was the rougher, more hilly ground over which the poacher had roamed, illicitly stalking Lord Weaver's deer.

It was a good place to doze, but I didn't feel sleepy. The confusion in my mind had grown worse; something was worrying me seriously, but I didn't know what it was. I tried to apply my godmother's method: question and answer; question and answer—but I couldn't put the right questions and I couldn't find any answers at all.

The confusion, I knew, would eventually clear itself; the struggle for clarification was going on and in time I would discover just what it was that was preying on my mind. It was a pity to waste the lovely day on useless mind-searching.

I was sitting so still that I must have seemed like part of the tree. A thrush flew down, surveyed me and decided that I was harmless and that I would not interrupt his meal. I didn't—but he looked so friendly that I turned slightly and edged sideways, stretching out a hand to see how near I could come without frightening him away.

And as I did so, the peace and silence were momentarily broken by a sudden, heavy thud—and although in that first instant I was completely unaware of what the sound meant, some

170

instinct kept me where I was. And then the realization of what I had heard came to me and brought me close to panic. With a swift gathering of all the forces of my body, I performed a half roll, a jerk and a spring—and reached safety behind the stout oak tree. As I did so, a second bullet thudded into the trunk against which I had been leaning. It landed at what—if I had still been sitting there—would have been shoulder height.. . heart height...

A wave of terror was making my limbs shake. I waited for it to recede; I was safe, I reminded myself; I had only to remain behind the tree; no bullet could reach me and all I had to do was decide how long it would be before I could safely emerge and inform Lord Weaver that a madman with a rifle was wandering round his grounds.

A crackling of twigs behind me sent me sick with renewed fear. I twisted round and peered through the thick undergrowth and saw that what I had taken to be level ground was in fact the bank of a stream. Climbing slowly up it, his air carefree, his lips pursed in a whistle, I saw James Maitland. I called to him sharply.

"Get down and stay down. Somebody's shooting."

I saw him turn an astonished face in my direction, but I was hidden from view. Whether he was a man who believed in taking no chances, or whether something in my voice communicated to him some of my own fear, I didn't know, but to my relief I saw him drop out of sight.

"I'm here, behind a tree," I called. "You're safe enough if

you crawl, but don't, whatever you do, show yourself."

His voice, wary and suspicious, reached me.

"If this is some kind of schoolgirl fun you're having—" he began.

"This isn't funny," I said. "There's a madman somewhere over there by the house and he's got a rifle."

There was no reply from the bank; a few moments later, I saw James's long, lean form snaking cautiously over the top. Still flat, he edged his way towards the bushes and began to push his way through them. When he joined me, his clothes were grey with dust and his hair full of leaves.

"Now," he demanded angrily, "what's it all about? I came out here to get some sleep, not to play Red Indians. What's this about shooting?"

I didn't answer. The fog that had settled on my brain was lifting. Question, answer; question, answer. I didn't need my godmother now. I had the thread and I was following it. Events were reassembling and, one by one, falling into place. There was no more disconnected sequence of events, of incidents; the picture was building up. I was thinking clearly and coldly, and at last I knew what had eluded me for so long.

I felt James put a hand under my chin and turn me to face him fully. His expression was puzzled and uneasy.

"Look here," he said with unusual gentleness, "there's nothing to be frightened about. You fell asleep and dreamt about the car back-firing. If there'd been shooting, I'd have heard it, wouldn't I? I was just over there by the river."

I could only stare at him speechlessly, my thoughts pursuing their orderly, relentless march. His hand moved to my shoulder and shook me roughly.

"Come on; snap out of it," he ordered.

At last I spoke.

"That silencer," I said.

"What the devil are you talking about?"

"The silencer. The one Lord Weaver said the poacher had on his rifle when they caught him. You can shoot without being heard."

"Anybody knows that. But the poacher's in prison and there aren't any bullets. Pull yourself together, will you, and take that look off your face. Nobody's shooting."

"Want me to prove it?" I asked.

I knew that nobody in or near the house could have seen him approach. I myself had walked slowly, openly, unsuspectingly across the open ground and as far as the unknown marksman knew, I was still alone. I was for the moment protected by my tree, but I would have to emerge sometime. I could, of course, crawl as James had crawled through the bushes and reach the river bank. But once there, unless I swam the river, I would have to come out on one side of the trees or the other—out into the open.

"I don't want you to prove anything," I heard James saying. "All I want you to do is get up and come back with me to the house."

I was wearing a light-coloured scarf round my head. I untied it and took it off; then I struggled out of the jacket of my suit. I draped the scarf round the shoulders and moved it slowly, very slowly out from the shelter in which we were crouching.

"If you're not feeling well—" I heard James beginning uneasily.

He said no more. The thud on the other side of the tree brought him up short and left him staring at me, his eyes blank with shock, his mouth hanging open. I tied the scarf round my head and put on my jacket, but still he stared at me open-mouthed.

"Don't try to talk with your mind full," I advised.

He closed his mouth, but his expression remained dazed.

"I don't understand," he said. "Are you trying to suggest—"

"I'm not trying to suggest anything," I said. "All I was trying to do was prove something."

"Prove what?"

"That somebody," I said quietly, "is trying to kill me."

Chapter Ten

James didn't speak for some time. He sat, dusty and leaf-crowned, looking long and steadily into my face—looking, I knew, for signs of hysteria or persecution-mania or just plain craziness. At the end of the survey, he spoke calmly.

"All right," he said. "As far as the eye can see, you're sane. As far as I know, you've got a good, steady head—too steady—and you don't suffer from hallucinations. What you've just said to me doesn't make any kind of sense, but I'm waiting to hear why you said it."

"Do you or do you not believe," I asked him, "that that bullet was intended for me?"

"Couldn't I keep an open mind?"

"No. If I'm to talk, I've got to talk to somebody who's prepared to believe what I say. I want to talk to somebody who knows me, who's known me for a long time; somebody who knows that I'm not the kind of person to whom this sort of thing should, could happen. You're prepared to listen, but you're not really prepared to believe."

"Who would be?" he asked reasonably. "Work it out for

175

yourself. For the past eighteen months or so you've been leading a dull, humdrum sort of life running after Madame. You might, of course, have been hiding from secret enemies—but you didn't have a hunted look. Now, from out of a nice, clear blue sky you announce that somebody's trying to kill you. Murder's a big word. If somebody's trying to kill you, they must have some reason for wanting to do it. Who would want to murder you—and for what?"

"Nobody, and for nothing," I answered. "I've got nothing in the world that anybody would want to murder me for."

"You've got a private income of sorts, haven't you?"

"Two hundred and forty pounds a year."

"I wouldn't murder anybody for two hundred and forty pounds a year. Have you ever done anybody any serious harm?"

"Not as far as I know."

"No enemies, and no reason for killing you. But you still think that somebody's got your number pinned up?"

"Yes, I do."

"Just because of these stray shots or not-stray shots?"

"No. It goes farther back than that."

"How far back?"

"Three weeks."

He calculated.

"Madame's birthday?"

"Yes."

176

"Oh now, wait a minute!" he protested. "You can't tell me those banisters weren't pretty shaky. How many times did I have my hand on them, going up and down from the kitchen. They—"

"They were shaky, but they were safe. If I hadn't made sure of that, would I have been fool enough to lean over them as often as I did? They were safe enough until the day I fell over them."

"You're seriously suggesting that somebody crept into the house with a saw, worked at the banisters when we were all going across the hall thinking of something else and—"

"Nobody needed a saw. When you go back to London, you can prove that by giving any part of those banisters four seconds of rough handling."

"Apart from banisters, what else?"

"Yesterday morning, when I left the hotel, I was nearly killed coming down that hill. The car brakes had gone wrong. Yesterday afternoon, a few moments after I had been standing on a small piece of ground on a hillside, a boulder crashed down and killed a man and would have killed me, too, if I'd stayed there a few minutes or a few seconds longer. This afternoon, I walked across this park alone and in full view and sat down with my back to this tree. Whoever's shooting can shoot straight. If I hadn't leaned over to try and touch a little thrush, I wouldn't be talking to you now. I haven't the remotest idea who could have anything against me, or who hates me enough to want to do me harm—but those things that happened were

177

not accidents. I accepted, at the time, the conclusion that the banisters had been giving way gradually. I realise that people whose car brakes fail don't go round imagining that somebody did it in order to kill them. Boulders do crash down hillsides and people do get killed—but whoever fired that rifle must have watched me coming across that park, must have waited till I sat down, must have taken careful and almost deadly aim. Now do you believe that somebody's trying to kill me?"

I stopped, and silence fell. James seemed to have nothing whatsoever to say.

"If you walked back to the house," I suggested after a time, "you could tell Lord Weaver that somebody—"

"Walk out of here?" he repeated in astonishment. "Not me! You've got me scared."

"They're not after you; they're after me. Are you going to sit here all the afternoon?"

The answer came promptly, but not from James. From across the park we heard the hideous sound of car horns sounded long and persistently.

"We've been missed," James said.

I looked across the park at the two gardeners who had obviously been sent in search of us.

"They're coming over to us" I said, and drew a long breath of relief.

"If you're planning to go back and talk about those bullets," James said, "don't."

178

I stared at him incredulously.

"What do you want me to do?" I demanded. "Walk back and say thank you for the nice party—and drive away?"

"Exactly that."

"You're out of your mind! Those bullets were fired from the house. In the gun-room—Lord Weaver told us so during lunch—there's the poacher's rifle with the silencer still on it. Somebody used that rifle and fired three shots at me. There'll be fingerprints. There'll be—"

"There'll be a hell of a fuss, there'll be a scare, there'll be a search, and at the end of it—what? They might find that the rifle had been fired. You'd show them the bullets in the tree—and then?"

"Then I'll tell them that this is the fourth attempt on—"

"Supposing it isn't? If the banisters were rotten, if the brakes were defective, what kind of hysterical little fool are you going to look?"

"But you've just seen—"

"I've just seen something that—tied on to other some-things—might amount to something. Alison, will you do something?"

"What?"

"Just trust me, that's all. Just give me twenty-four hours."

I said nothing. His terse summary of the probable results of reporting the incident to Lord Weaver had made me see the situation in a new and almost hopeless light.

179

I saw James, still keeping behind the shelter of the tree, put out his long legs, cross them, lean back and close his eyes.

"Those two chaps are coming this way," he said. "They'll see my legs and they'll come up to this tree and I'm not moving away from it until they do. When they arrive, I'll have fallen asleep and you will have forgotten what the time was."

The two men began to call as they came towards us.

"Mr. Maitland, Mr. Maitland!"

When the two sturdy bodies halted, forming a screen, James appeared to wake with a start from a peaceful doze. He got quickly to his feet and gave a startled glance at his watch.

"Good heavens!" he exclaimed. "Is that the time?"

"They're waiting for you, sir," one of the men told him. "Have you seen Miss Sinclair anywhere?"

"I'm here," I said, and stood up. "Is everybody ready to go?"

They had been ready, we were told, for almost a quarter of an hour.

"Go ahead and tell them we're on our way," directed James.

He brushed the dust from his clothes and the leaves from his hair; then we followed the two men, keeping as much as possible directly behind them. It was foolish and cowardly, but reassuring.

As we came within sight of the others, we saw Oskar and Christina driving away. Mr. Bernstein waited only to say good-bye to us and then drove away promising to await us in Edinburgh. Madame, standing on the wide stone steps, was talking to Lord and Lady Weaver.

Neil was walking towards Eden's car when James called him back.

"Look, will you drive Madame's car?" he asked. "I'd like to take Alison—just for a change."

"We're going straight through to Edinburgh," Neil told him curtly. "We're all tired of this cattle drive. It was your idea and it was a bad one and the sooner we all get to Edinburgh and back on the job, the better."

"Well, I'll drive Alison to Edinburgh," James said.

There was a pause. I saw Neil's eyes on us, hard and cold and speculative. Before he answered, the door of Eden's car opened and Margaret came over and stood beside us.

"If James wants to take Alison," she said, "I'll go with Neil in Madame's car. Eden can drive alone for a change."

Neil turned to face her. He said nothing, but I had the odd feeling that a message passed between them. Then he turned and spoke to James.

"I'll take the Great North road as far as Barlinks," he said. "Just out of there there's a place called the Legion Inn. We'll wait for you there. It's about two hours' run; make the most of them."

"Thanks," James said.

We delayed a moment longer in order to apologise to

Lord and Lady Weaver for our disappearance, and to say our thanks and farewells; then we were following the other cars down the long avenue of beeches. But when we reached the main road, James did not follow them to the left. Instead, he halted until they were out of sight, and then drove swiftly and unhesitatingly to the right.

"Your compass isn't working," I said.

I tried to keep my tone light, but he heard the quaver in it and turned to glance at me. He saw the tears pouring down my face, but he said nothing; he settled down in his seat and I saw the speedometer needle begin to move steadily.

We went on and on and on. James was driving within the safety margin, but only just within. I knew that we were headed south, but I didn't know where we were going. All I knew, with unspeakable thankfulness, was that for the moment we had left bullets behind. I sat still, trying to find reasons for what had happened—but I could find no reasons. Waves of panic rose in me and then slowly, sickeningly subsided.

"Whenever you have to stop," I heard James say, "let me know."

"Now," I said.

He went on for a little while and then drew the car to the side of the road, just beyond a telephone box. We both got out. When I walked back to the car, James was telephoning.

"I rang up the Legion Inn," he said, rejoining me and driving on. "I left a message for Patterson, telling him we'd be delayed."

"Where are we going?" I asked.

He made no answer; he had stopped the car at a small wayside shop. He went inside and came out carrying three bulging paper bags. He put them on to my lap and I saw that they contained pears, bananas and apples.

"You'll have to make those do," he said, when we were once more on our way. "We haven't time to stop for food. I'll buy you a drink later."

"Where are we going?"

"We're going to London—but not to see the Queen." He passed out of the built-up zone; the car shot forward and the speedometer began its rapid climb. "We're going to London because London was where it all began. If we're going to get any further with this thing, we've got to start working on facts and not on fancies. Falling over those banisters was either an accident or not an accident—and that's the first thing we're going to find out."

It was dark when we reached the house in Cranston Avenue. I put my hand on the handle of the car door as it stopped, but James checked me.

"No, not you. You'll stay here," he directed.

He was fishing in his pocket for a key. The house was unlighted. He went up the steps and after a few moments I saw the light go up in the hall. After what seemed a long time, it went out again. The hall door opened and closed and James

183

came running down the steps and got into the car.

"Well?" I asked as he turned the car.

"I'll submit a report in due course," he said. "Our next stop is the Thomas's."

He allowed me eight minutes to have a drink at a snack bar and to buy a supply of sandwiches. We ate them as we drove northward through the darkness. The streets were clearer; driving was easier. We flew through the night, James still and intent and concentrated at the wheel.

"I can drive if you want me to," I offered.

"No, thanks."

We didn't go up to the hotel. James stopped outside the garage and sounded the horn—once, twice and then again.

"I phoned old Tom," he told me. "He said he'd come down and talk to me."

We sat in the darkness for about five minutes, and then we saw the headlights of a car on the hill. It drew up beside us and old Tom and young Tom got out. James walked across to speak to them and then old Tom unlocked the door of the garage and the three men went inside.

When they came out, James checked old Tom as he started forward to speak to me.

"Not now," he said. "There's no time. We'll be back, Tom."

He got into the car and we said good-bye to old Tom and to young Tom and then we drove on into the night. I didn't have to ask where we were going next.

I felt sick and my head was throbbing with a loud, persistent beat: *Why, why, why?*

"Try to sleep" I heard James say.

I didn't want to sleep. My eyes, like his, were fixed strainingly on the road ahead—but sometime later they must have closed...

I woke to the loveliness of a huge round moon that was flooding the countryside with light. My head was on James's shoulder. I raised it stiffly.

"Three o'clock in the morning" he said. "My mother used to sing a song about it. Hungry?"

"No."

"I could eat a horse, tail and all."

We passed all-night cafes, but he did not stop. The car sped on, now past a sleeping town, now between fields that lay bathed in moonlight. I knew where we were. I looked out for the Motel, half expecting to see even at this hour some sign of life—but when we reached it, there was none; a lighted notice at the entrance stated somewhat brusquely that no more accommodation was available.

"Pity," commented James. "We didn't need accommodation, but we could have done with some coffee and sandwiches."

He had slowed down and soon he had to reduce our pace still further, for we had turned into the narrow, rocky road along which I had driven with Neil—when? Yesterday?

I shivered and James sent me a questioning glance.

"Cold?"

"No."

"Frightened?"

"Yes."

"So am I, if you're interested. If there's a war round the corner, I'm not going to prove one of its heroes."

"You've got nothing to be afraid of," I told him.

He did not answer. He had reached the place at which we had lunched the day before. He stopped the car and switched off the engine and an eerie silence enveloped us. I knew that we were both seeing a circle of cars, a group of people, a chauffeur serving food.

"You needn't have driven down here," I said.

"You mean that what I came to see was at the top of the hill and not down here? That's true—but I want to retrace your steps. You're coming with me and you're going to lead me to that viewpoint you found. Come on."

We got out of the car. In silence I led him up the narrow slope.

"I'm only an amateaur," I heard James saying behind me. "Even the most junior investigator would have remembered to bring along a torch. When you're a grandmother reciting this tale to your grandchildren, just tell them I knew there was going to be a full moon."

When we reached the point at which I had broken through the bushes, he put me aside.

"Let me," he said. "I'm not wearing nylons."

He pushed a way through and I followed him and soon we were standing on the little grassy shelf. Walking to its edge, we stood looking down at the rocks upon which the drunk old man had died.

James turned towards the steps. He put out a hand and I took it and he pulled me up boulder by boulder until at last we stood together on the top of the hill. My heart was beating violently and I found it hard to breathe, but it was not the ascent that had made me breathless.

We had come out on to a narrow tableland. I saw James walk cautiously to the edge of it and peer downward. He seemed to me to stand there for a very long time. He spoke at last without turning.

"Come here."

I went forward slowly and stood beside him.

"As you see," he said, "anybody standing here could have seen you clearly. They wouldn't have seen the old man, because he was sitting over to the left and that bush over there would have hidden him. But even if he'd been in sight, what's one murder more or less?"

"You said that murder was a big word," I reminded him.

"And so it is."

"But—"

187

"But what?"

"Nobody was alone up here. A number of people were wandering about. The bandsmen could have walked over here. To do a thing like this, people need time—time to think, time to plan. How, with all those people so close, could it have been anything more than an accident?"

"Like this," said James.

He took my arm and drew me aside. All around us were boulders, sizeable but not immovable. Still holding my arm, he put a foot under the one nearest to us, scraped to and fro for a moment in the soil to get a toe-hold, and then without any visible effort levered the boulder from its place. It turned over once, stopped—and then, swiftly, James leaned over and with his free hand sent it on its way over the edge. There was the tearing sound of twigs, a thud, a pause and then the noise of rock meeting rock.

"Murder," James said reflectively into the ensuing silence, "is easier than you'd think. Not a big boulder—but down on that narrow little ledge, there's no hope of getting out of its way."

There was silence, and I realised that he was giving me time.

"Ready for it?" he asked quietly at last.

"Yes."

"Then here it is. Somebody had tampered with the banisters. Somebody had tampered with those brakes. When I say tampered, I mean of course that they were deliberately—"

I didn't hear the end of the sentence. I was some way away, being violently sick. When I went towards James once more, my knees were shaking so much that I could hardly walk. He came to meet me and, taking my arm in a firm grip, led me down the path towards the car. He opened the door on my side, but I was shivering all over and the effort of lifting a foot to step into the car seemed too much. Without a word, he stooped and swung me off my feet and put me gently against the blue cushions.

I would have given anything in the world to have regained control over my limbs, but something inside me seemed to have snapped. After watching me for a few moments, he walked round and took his place at the wheel and the car began the slow journey back to the road.

I was still shaking when he stopped some time later at an all-night cafe by the roadside. Drawn up on a clearing beside it were two enormous trucks; their drivers were standing at a brightly-lit hatch in front of the cafe, eating and drinking. James went inside the building and came back with a tray on which there were two cups of steaming coffee and two plates of hot stew made with meat and potatoes and vegetables. Propped against each plate were huge hunks of bread. He put the tray on a long bare trestle table nearby, picked up one of the cups of coffee and came over to stand beside me.

"I'll hold it till you've got some of it inside you," he said.

Slowly, patiently, he held it to my lips and steadied it as

I took sip after sip. It was hot and strong and sweet. When I had drunk a little, James reached with his free hand into the pocket of the car and pulled out a flask. He took the stopper off with his teeth and poured a generous measure of brandy into my coffee. Then he held the cup to my lips again and I drank it to the end. He took the empty cup away and came back with a plate of stew; his other hand held one of the large squares of bread.

"Don't worry about your weight," he counselled. "Can you hold the plate?"

I nodded. The shaking had stopped. Now and then I shuddered violently, but my feeling of helpless panic had passed. I had never in my life known what it was to give way completely, and shame welled up in me.

James thrust a spoon into my hand.

"Here, eat with this," he said, "and drop the bread in and mop up all that nice rich gravy. I was a fool to let you go so long without stoking."

He stood beside me, eating and drinking. We finished our plates of stew and he went in to get them refilled; we finished the second helpings and then ate ham sandwiches and drank more coffee. Life began to flow back into me, and courage, and with them came a sense of almost overpowering gratitude towards James.

He went in to pay the bill and I got out of the car and went across to a grimy little hut with a crookedly-hung door labelled, hopefully, *Ladies*. I went inside and in spite of the single cold-water tap, the greasy basin and the cracked glass, emerged feeling cleaner and fresher and almost back to normal.

James was nowhere to be seen. I sat in the car and waited for him and presently he came out and climbed cautiously in beside me—the space between the steering wheel and his stomach, he explained, had lessened considerably.

We drove away, but now we were driving more slowly.

"All you need now," James said, "is a good sleep. A real sleep."

"I'd rather talk."

"Then talk. Tell me who's trying to murder you."

"I can't think *who,"* I said. 'All I can think is why, why, *why?"*

"The why might lead to the who," he said, "but in most cases of this kind, the first thing a person wants to know is who's trying to finish them off."

"All I can think," I said desperately "is that it's some terrible mistake. Nobody could want to kill me. Nobody's got any reason to kill me."

He brought the car to a stop and I turned to look at him questioningly.

"Dawn," he explained, and jerked his chin to the right. "Dawn. When I see the first faint signs of dawn, I always like to stop and haul up my flag for the day that's coming."

He turned in his seat to face me fully. "Having hauled it

up," he went on, "I wouldn't like to see it flying at half mast on your account. Will you drive up with me, here and now, straight to your godmother's?"

"Without going back to the others?"

"Without going back to the others. Hasn't it struck you yet that among those others is the man or the woman—or both—who's trying to murder you? Why go back and let them have another go? Why not drive on with me to this gracious god-mother of yours and take shelter behind her skirts?"

"If somebody's trying to kill me, what's to prevent them from following me up to my godmother's?"

"Nothing at all—but by that time, we'll have told the story to the police."

"The police!"

"P-o-l-i-c-e." James spelt it out. "The fellows with the blue lamp. They never call them in in books—or not very often. Instead, some clever chap who's read Sherlock Holmes takes up the whole of the last chapter telling you what you'd guessed on page three. But I don't want to go into business as a private investigator. I've told you already—I'm scared. I'm scared on your account, and now that I'm in this, I'm scared on my own account. The sooner I see a nice burly bobby under a tall blue helmet, the happier I'll be."

"To go up to my godmother's"—I was speaking slowly, trying to picture it—"to arrive without luggage, to arrive with a stranger in a stranger's car after having been away so long, to walk in and tell her that somebody's trying to murder me..."

"She might think, for a moment or two, that you were a bad nervous case," James agreed, "but remember that I'll be there too. Remember that I saw those banisters. Remember that I talked to old Tom and to young Tom about those brakes. Up on that hill, I gave you a demonstration of how easy it was for somebody to push a boulder over. The 4B murder: banisters, brakes, boulders, bullets. The police might discount a lot of what I told them, but they'd have to listen to old Tom."

"If you run away," I said "you like to know what you're running away from."

"Madame, Mr. Bernstein, Oskar, Christina—and your three old chums." He looked at me for some moments in silence. "You wouldn't talk about it before," he said. "Suppose you talk about it now? There's a story, isn't there?"

"Not much of a story."

"It sounds like an old one: Two men and a girl."

"No, it wasn't that."

"Were you in love with Croft?"

"Yes. Desperately."

"All right. Let's have it."

"He came up to Edinburgh to play the lead in *Seascape*. D'you know it?"

"I know it. He must have been good in that part."

"He was. I was twenty-four and I'd never been in love. I don't think anybody was ever as happy as I was when I met

193

Eden three days later at a party and believed that whatever had happened to me had happened to him too."

"Two less likely subjects for love at first sight I never saw," James commented. "Pray continue."

"I took him home to meet my godmother. Margaret was away—she was away a good deal, as I told you. I wrote to her and made her promise to come back in time for the wedding.

"It was January—a terrible month in Edinburgh, but I didn't notice it. I knew that my godmother didn't like Eden; I was sorry, but it didn't seem to matter much.

"The wedding was fixed for the fourteenth of February— St. Valentine's day; my birthday.—My name's Alison Valentine. Three weeks before the wedding, Margaret came home. One small item in the other innumerable items of news she told me was that Neil Patterson would soon be coming home to visit his parents. He and Margaret had met at Zermatt, ski-ing, and had travelled back to London together.

"I didn't dream that Neil would come to the house—but I'd forgotten that there were two things to bring him in spite of the dislike that he and I felt for one another. One thing was that he and Margaret had enjoyed meeting again. The other thing was that he and Eden were very old friends. So ten days after Margaret came home, Neil Patterson walked across the fields that separated our houses, and came in unannounced. We were in the library, the four of us—Margaret and Eden and my godmother and me. We were sitting at a tea table in front of a big log fire."

194

I closed my eyes. I could see the door opening. I could see our heads turning. I could see him in the doorway, carelessly, almost insolently at ease ...

"You were in the library," I heard James say, "and Patterson came in."

"Yes. If I was telling anybody else this part of the story, they wouldn't believe it—but you know Neil and you know that it's true. He came in and we talked—I don't know what about. All I could think of was the way he'd looked at Eden, and at me, when he was standing in the doorway. I couldn't have explained, even to myself, why I had a feeling that something was wrong... something was going wrong. He went away, but before going, he asked Eden to walk home with him. Eden came back two hours later—and in those two hours with Neil, everything that had been between us had been swept away.

"I never saw Eden at my godmother's house again. He sent me a letter saying that he was sorry to have hurt me but that he had mistaken his feelings. A little later, I learnt that he and Margaret were seeing one another. I don't know exactly what I did the day I heard that. I went out and walked about the streets, I think. When I came home, Margaret was waiting for me. We didn't say much. She loved Eden, Eden loved her, and that was all, and they were both desperately sorry...

"They say that when you're unhappy, you should do some work. The work I did before leaving home was packing and returning all my wedding presents. Then I said good-bye and told my godmother I'd rather stay away for a while. She asked where I was going and I said I'd write and give her my address. And that," I ended, "is the story. I never saw them again until Neil and I met on the day of your arrival in London. If there's anything in anything I've said that makes you feel that Eden or Margaret or Neil have any reason to murder me, I'd like to know what it is."

There was a long silence.

"You still believe," James said at last, "that Patterson did that out of hate?"

"How could it have been anything else? I hadn't seen him since I was eleven. I was no Lolita; I had a mean disposition, straggly hair and a sarcastic tongue that every boy in the neighbourhood was terrified of. Could he have cherished that image throughout the years? We were old enemies. Perhaps he saw as soon as he came into that room that Margaret was in love with Eden; all he had to do during the walk home was to explain to Eden that he could change his mind even so near the day of the wedding. You know that he can manage Eden. You've seen him do it."

"He tried to harm you then; he might be trying to harm you now," said James. "But why Eden and Margaret, having got one another—even though they don't appear to like what they've got—should want to do you any harm, I can't figure out."

"So you see," I said, "it isn't who. It's *why.*"

In the dawning light, we looked at one another. We both knew that what we had shared in the night had brought us very close together. James put out a finger and laid it on my cheek and rubbed it gently up and down.

"I wish I were one of those bulldog characters," he said. "I wish I had a whole lot of courage and grit—then I could give you some of it. I have a feeling you're going to need it."

I put up a hand and imprisoned his and laid it against my cheek.

"Thank you for last night and this morning," I said. "I'm sorry I went to pieces."

"You can go to pieces any time you like—any time I'm around."

We sat in silence, our hands clasped loosely.

"You make it so difficult, Alison," he said after a time. "With most people, you could find—if you looked hard enough—some sort of reason for murder. But with you... you're not the victim type, somehow. You're beautiful, but you're not the lush sexy sort that runs into trouble. You're not provocative. You're honest and down to earth and—I was going to say pure, but it's a dead word. There's something about you that makes people think of nice fresh things like primroses and honey and dew on the grass and lovely dawns like this one." He paused. "Are you frightened?"

"Yes," I said. "Like you. But I don't want to go to my godmother's. Not yet."

"You want to go back to the others?"

"Yes. I'm not frightened of them, somehow. It doesn't

197

make sense to me to think of any one of them as a possible murderer."

Once again there was silence.

"Well, we're going back," James said. "I don't want to go, but if you're going, I'm going."

"Thank you," I said. "I'll feel better if I know that you're there."

We came together and clung together there in the dawn. For mutual protection, James said.

Chapter Eleven

We got to the Legion Inn at noon on what was to prove the hottest day of the year. Although only a hundred yards off the Great North Road, the building had a blessedly cool, remote look, and as we drove up we glimpsed through the trees a green lawn on which were small tables and coloured umbrellas. We passed under the inn's sign which was suspended across the drive; James slowed down to examine it and at last decided that it was meant to be Hannibal on an elephant crossing the Alps.

I looked at the line of cars standing outside the inn. Among them I saw Madame's and Eden's.

We got out and James nodded towards the lawn.

"Over there's the most likely place to find them on a day like this," he said. "Let's go and get it over with."

I walked beside him across the grass. His hands were in his pockets; his pace was calm and unhurried and he looked as though he had enjoyed a night's sound sleep. There were four of them waiting—Madame and Margaret, Eden and Neil. We saw their heads turn towards us; it could not be said that their expressions were cordial. As we approached and the two men got to their feet, I realised that I had prepared no sort of explanation for our long absence. The truth couldn't be told, and there seemed nothing else to say.

But James was saying it at some length. It was foolish, he said regretfully, to have allowed the car to run out of petrol. It was even more foolish to have left me in the car and trudged across several fields to a farmhouse with the idea of waking the owners and asking if they had a spare can to sell him. When he'd calmed the dogs sufficiently to be able to climb down the tree again, it was to find a night-capped old harridan peering at him from an upper window. Yes, there was a can of petrol, she had informed him; yes, he could have it if he paid for it—but he would have to wait until she put something on and could come down and get it for him. Instead of getting it for him, she had telephoned to the police and they hadn't believed a word of the petrol story until he had led them to the spot at which he thought he had left me—but it was one thing to leave a car on an empty stretch of road, and quite another thing to find it again. By which time, it was dawn and even the police needed breakfast.

Halfway through this recital, he was left talking to himself. Madame, turning to me, told me in one brief sentence that she would accept my notice and I could go whenever I pleased. Neil got up and walked away, and Margaret moved over to take the vacant seat beside me.

"The car didn't crash?" she asked.

"No."

"Something happened, Alison. You look like death. Can I do anything?"

"I'm all right, thanks."

She left it at that, but her eyes remained anxiously on my face. I heard Eden addressing me.

"You must have come a long way round," he said dryly.

"—and there was this toothless old witch," droned James, "trying to make out that I'd—"

"It's always a mistake," Eden went on, "to upset Neil seriously. In view of the fact that the success of this play hangs more or less on him, perhaps you would have been wiser to have got back last night."

I looked at Madame. There was a long, cool drink on the table in front of her; she was holding a straw and jabbing viciously at the thin slice of lemon in the glass, now and then scowling up at James as he delivered his monologue. Our eyes met and I saw for an instant, before she looked away, dislike mingled with a kind of curiosity, as if she were reassessing my character.

I began to feel a little dizzy. The day was breathlessly hot; although I had taken off the jacket of my suit, the light woollen jersey I was wearing seemed as heavy as a plaid. James had stopped talking and was ordering drinks, but his voice seemed to be coming from a distance. Seated here in this brilliant sunshine, it was impossible to believe that last night we had spoken of murder. Margaret beside me, Madame a few feet away lifting her drink and bending to put her lips to the straw, Eden stubbing out a cigarette, Neil walking slowly across the grass to rejoin us. ..

I had sometimes had bad dreams, but I could not remember ever having experienced a nightmare. Until now. A nightmare, I realised, must be this horrifying mixture of the common-place and the incredible. A sunny day, groups of people seated at tables round a lawn, white-jacketed waiters, self-possessed women and relaxed-looking men—and beneath this pleasant surface, deep, nameless horrors. Noon sunshine—and dawn on a chilly roadside with a man and a woman talking of mur-der . ..

"Alison, would you like to come and rest in my room?" Margaret asked.

I shook my head. Madame's cold, angry eyes came round to rest on my face. But she made no comment, and a moment later Neil reached us and dropped a paper on the table in front of James.

"Hotel bill," he said briefly. "When you and Alison didn't show up, we decided to stay the night and wait till you did. I paid it; you can pay me."

James folded the bill and slipped it into his pocket.

"It'll come out of the profits," he said.

I was watching a woman who was strolling back towards the hotel swinging a wet bathing-suit. The thought of cool water made the heat almost unbearable, and I decided to get my suitcase from Madame's car and find a cloakroom in which I could change into a cool dress.

"Where are people swimming?" James asked. "In the river?"

"There's a swimming-pool," Margaret said. "Rather a nice one."

James got to his feet.

"Then that's where anybody can find me for the next three quarters of an hour," he stated.

"It is only for residents," Madame told him coldly. "You cannot go."

"In my bathing-trunks, they won't be able to tell the difference," James assured her.

"I'll come with you," Margaret said, and rose. She looked at me. "How about you, Alison?"

"No bathing-suit," I said.

"My spare one will fit you." There was a perceptible pause before she added: "Coming, Eden?"

Nothing ever felt better than the water of the pool when I dived in a quarter of an hour later. I swam under water to the deep end, surfaced, and shook the water out of my eyes to find that James had followed me along the side and was regarding me with astonishment.

"That's swimming," he said admiringly, and dived in to join me.

The pool was beautifully laid out. God himself, James said, treading water, couldn't have made it look more natural. Beginning as an orthodox rectangle, it flowed on between sloping grassy banks, curving like a river, widening to form a small, circular, tree-edged pool, curving again to end at last against another green bank. Nothing was to be seen from the water but trees and flowering shrubs and cleverly-placed flower-beds.

"Most outdoor pools look inviting enough in summer," James commented, "but they give you the shivers all the rest of the year. This way, it's an all-year-round attraction—swimming or scenic."

As he was speaking, a man of about my own age pushed rudely between us. Having made certain that we were looking at him, he broke into an almost professional freestyle. On an impulse, I followed him. As I came level, he saw me and increased his pace, and it became a not-too-friendly race. If I hadn't been out of practice, I would have passed him before I did, but I left him behind at last, and swam back slowly, feeling rather ashamed of my exhibition.

Swimming in the same direction was Eden and I passed him too, and remembered the day in a friend's indoor pool when he had challenged me and I had beaten him. I remembered clearly the surprise, the first stab of doubt I had felt when I realised that he had not liked being beaten. The only thing I could do well, I had found myself explaining to him, was swim.

And then I remembered that marriage with Margaret must have meant being beaten not only at swimming, but perhaps at skiing and tennis and golf too, and even at shooting...

Shooting...

I swam to the bank and clambered up it, not feeling the sharp stones that cut into my knees. I turned to look at her. She was on her back floating idly, easily, her lovely body outlined in its clinging wet green suit.

Shooting. ..

The nightmare was returning. Eden and Neil were standing by the pool and I could see their reflections in the water, dancing dizzily like the thoughts in my brain. I slid back into the water, dislodging a small shower of stones, and as my head cleared, I thought with horror of the change that had taken place in me in the past twenty-four hours. To think of Margaret attempting to harm me was like believing that my godmother could bring herself to hurt me.

The utter impossibility of this thought did more than anything else to steady me. Eden could shoot, and Neil. So could James and a great many other men I had met.

But Eden and Margaret, I remembered, had spent their honeymoon at the Weavers' house. They would at least know their way round it.

One ... or both ...

Today, I remembered with a surge of happiness, I would be at home with my godmother. Today, after all the long months, I would be in my own room, sleep in my own bed, wake to look out over the rose garden and the neat paths and the hedges and fields and hills beyond. I needed to be at home. Home was shelter. Home was safety.

I felt suddenly free from fear. The long, secure years that stretched behind me filled me with confidence for the future. If I wanted to stay at home indefinitely, I could stay; she loved me and she would be glad. She was old; perhaps there weren't too many years left for us to be together.

Thinking of her, I swam slowly round a curve of the pool.

"Lunch," James said as I passed him. "Real food on a real table."

"Coming," I called back.

I saw him clamber out of the pool and put on a shabby bathrobe. There were no other swimmers in sight; lunch, it was clear, had called to all the other bathers as loudly as it had done to James.

I quickened my pace. I would swim on to the end of the pool and then back, and get out and change for lunch. I hadn't been in a swimming pool for a long, long time and I felt strangely reluctant to leave it. I swam slowly on my side, putting out a hand to touch the restless reflections on the water. Then I turned on my back and gazed up at the cloudless sky, and reminded myself that this was all very well and I was enjoying it, but if I had to choose between sunny swimming pools and blue-grey, mist-shrouded Scottish hills I wouldn't hesitate long. The hills of home. I swam round the last curve,

206

did a swift turn under water and kicked to surface for the return swim.

But I didn't surface.

My eyes were open, and even before the hand gripped me, I saw it through the pale green, quivering water. Then it was on my shoulder pressing me down, down ...

I twisted violently, felt the hand slide off me—and then two hands closed about my throat.

Down and down—but not too far down. My senses were becoming blurred, but I understood well enough why I wouldn't be forced any deeper. Only one of us was in the water, would remain under the green dancing water to the end while the hands reached down from the grassy slope.

With a last, desperate effort, I doubled up, and straightened—and my feet met yielding flesh and for a moment, the hands loosed their grip. In one second I was at the bank, my arm out, clutching at the grass—and then the hands were forcing me down again, down into the water.

There was no more struggle. The hands were on my shoulders, pressing. I could only reach up helplessly, feebly, in a last attempt to force them away. And as I did so, I realised that I was holding something in my right hand. A stone—small, but sharply pointed, I knew, for it had torn across my own body.

I managed to reach upwards, backwards. I struck once...

The hands were no longer there. I was free and clinging to the bank, choking. I drew in long, gasping breaths and then dragged myself up and lay face downwards while wave after wave of nausea passed over me. There were sounds close by, but I could not identify them—until at last I raised my head and saw the struggling forms of two men.

At the moment that I identified them, they went down with a crash on the sloping bank and rolled to the edge of the water. Then James, who was uppermost, got slowly to his feet—but Neil lay where he was, his eyes closed. On one side of his forehead, I saw a wound from which blood was slowly trickling.

Chapter Twelve

It was not possible, for some time, to speak. James, stepping over Neil's unconscious body, came and knelt beside me, holding me in his arms, his body shaking.

"Are you ... all right?" he brought out at last.

"Yes."

He lifted me in his arms and moved me out of the shadows to the sunshine farther up the bank. I stared stupidly at the blood on Neil's forehead, and then I made a move towards him, only to feel James's hand on my arm, checking me.

"No," he said. "Let the swine be."

I turned slowly to look at him and something he saw in my face made him lean forward and lay his cheek against mine.

"It's over," he said, in a low, crooning voice. "No more. Don't look like that, Alison. Don't, don't."

I lay in his arms, my cheek against rough, torn towelling, my hands clutching his long, hard, bony fingers. Close by, Neil lay motionless, his checked shirt and flannel trousers undamaged in the struggle, his feet in sandals, his wet hair scarcely disarranged. The minutes went by and nothing disturbed the silence. At last I stirred and freed myself and spoke shakily.

"What happened?"

"I got out of the pool and walked towards the hotel. I didn't see Neil or Eden, but I remembered seeing them get out some time before me, and I guessed they were inside, changing. Margaret was walking some way ahead of me. She turned and waited for me and we walked on together and then she asked where you were. I said you were coming; I told her to go on and I'd wait for you. I waited, but you didn't come, and I began to feel annoyed, because I was getting chilly. I shouted, but there was no answer. I wondered if it would be more sensible to go on and change and wait for you in the bar, so I began to walk away—and then I stopped, not because I was frightened of anything in particular, but because I remembered that it was always better to be sure than to be sorry. So I turned and walked back.

"You weren't in the near end of the pool, and that worried me a bit, because you'd had ample time to swim back to it. I walked round the first curve; I couldn't see you and I began to walk faster—but even then I wasn't too worried. I suppose I couldn't bring myself to believe, in spite of the evidence, that you were in danger. They'd looked so harmless there, the three of them, sitting at that table. Angry, but harmless. The only one that looked dangerous was Madame. But when I went round another curve of the pool and still couldn't see you, I found myself running. I think I began shouting, but I can't be sure. Then I think I must have lost my head completely because I can't remember what happened when I rounded that last bend and saw you ... and him. His hands were on you and you were under the water—hanging limply; so much I could see. He was bending over you and I don't remember any more until I was on him, dragging him away. I wanted to kill him. I've never wanted to kill anybody before—but I wanted to kill him at that moment."

There was silence. Once I shivered, and James began to rub my body with rough, swift hands.

"I can't leave you," he said "in case he comes round while I'm away. I can't take you with me in case he comes round and tries to get away. We've got to—"

He stopped. Neil had stirred. We heard him give a low moan, and for some moments longer he lay still. Then his eyes opened to the blue, cloudless sky and he stared up at it, at first blankly and then with a dawning realisation of where he was. He struggled to a sitting position and James got up.

"On your feet," he said.

Neil stared up at him, and into his eyes came a look of such horror that I found myself getting up and going to stand beside James.

"I hit you and knocked you out," James said in the same quiet, deathly cold voice. 'I'll do it again—if I have to."

Neil did not seem to hear. He was getting slowly to his feet. He stood looking from side to side, and something in his eyes—a look of dread—kept us silent. At last he faced James.

"Eden... Where's Eden?" he asked urgently. "For God's sake, where's Eden?"

"Eden?" James echoed the name blankly. "I don't know where Eden is. All I know is that—"

He stopped. In the terrible silence that followed, the three of us stared at one another.

It was Neil who first turned and walked down the slope and looked down at the gently-moving pale green water. James followed him. I don't know how long it was before I summoned the courage to go and stand beside them and look down into the tree-shadowed depths...

Slowly, stiffly, James turned to stare at Neil.

"Then Eden" he began—and stopped.

"Yes," Neil said. "Eden."

A stone rolled slowly down the bank and fell with a soft splash into the water. The pool's surface quivered, but the body lying in the green depths was stilled for ever.

Eden's body was carried to a room in a small, empty annexe of the hotel. James and Neil dealt with all the formalities.

Madame, lunching alone, heard the stir as news of the tragedy spread among the guests; a kindly old lady at last told her as gently as possible that one of her young friends—the actor, Eden Croft—had been found drowned in the swimming-pool.

This, and other matters, I learned only later. For I was with Margaret in her bedroom, the door closed against the inquisitive or the ghoulish. She was lying on the bed, her eyes closed, her face chalk-white. There had been, as yet, no questions; I knew that they must come and that I must answer them as Neil had told me to answer.

We weren't dressed for tragedy. We were still wearing our bathing suits; over hers was a short primrose-coloured robe; over mine was a thick sweater belonging to James. I could see us both in the long glass fixed to the wall, our hair wild, our limbs shaking.

James walked in after a token knock, and his anger, when he saw us, went a good deal of the way towards steadying us. He dragged warm clothes from Margaret's cupboard, threw them at us and told us that he would give us ten minutes to get into them. When he returned, he was followed by a waiter pushing a heavily-laden wagon; he tipped the man, pulled the wagon into the bedroom and shut the door.

"Haven't we got enough to think of," he demanded, "without adding pneumonia? Here—sit down and get this inside you both."

He watched us drinking cups of hot soup and then, suddenly realising his own hunger, shared the rest of the food into three portions. Nobody spoke; it was enough to feel warmth and strength returning to our cold bodies. When Margaret pushed her food away, James in grim silence pushed it back, and she forced it down. The looking-glass told me that we were looking less pallid.

I asked where Neil was, and James's only answer was to

213

redirect my attention to my food.

"Later," he said.

A waiter came in, took away the wagon and left us a jug of hot coffee.

"Where is Neil?" Margaret asked when we had drunk it.

"Dealing with the officials. Ringing up your mother. Ringing up the rest of the cast. Ringing up theatres. Eden left more than one gap."

He spoke the name naturally, calmly. Margaret's eyes came round to rest on him, and he continued in the same factual tone.

"There'll be a lot for you to go through," he told her, "but we'll spare you all we can. Sitting about shivering in a wet bathing suit isn't going to prepare you for any ordeals."

"No," she agreed quietly. "James—"

"Well?"

His voice was gentle, but it was some time before she spoke again.

"Did Eden ... did he ..."

He waited, and she realised that he was not going to help her and that it was better that he should not. She spoke clearly and steadily.

"Eden was a good swimmer."

"The best swimmers can get cramp," James said.

"Do you think he got cramp?"

"I think that's what the verdict will be at the inquest. I my-

214

self think that he was doing an underwater turn at the end of the pool, and went too close into the side. There was a bruise on the side of his head—enough to stun him, enough to send him down. When I went back to Alison, when Neil walked down to see where we were, we didn't know-how could we know?—that Eden was in the water. When we saw him, it was too late. I'm sorry, Margaret—but that's the last time I'll say it. Eden's dead and doesn't need anybody any more, but Neil is alive and in bad shape, and he'll need all the help we can give him. Now I'm going to take Alison away while you rest. Lock your door; don't answer any knocks—especially Madame's knocks. Try to sleep. If you want to talk later, I'll let you—but not now." He dragged the bedclothes back, found her dressing-gown and handed it to her.

"Right into the bed. You won't get much rest later—get what you can now."

He drew me out of the room and we waited in the corridor until we heard Margaret turn the key in the lock. Then he took my arm in a firm grasp and led me towards a flight of stairs.

"Where are we going?" I asked.

"Up to Neil's room. He's waiting for you."

Neil opened the door. He seemed to have aged ten years in the past two hours.

"Come in," he said.

He pushed a low chair towards me and I sat down. James walked to the window; Neil stood by a table in the middle of

215

the room, gazing unseeingly at the miscellany of articles on it—an ash-tray, a little bone elephant, a bowl of hideous artificial flowers.

"Is Margaret all right?" he asked.

"Yes," James answered.

"Do you think she knows anything?"

"No, I don't. There might be one or two items she can't tie up, but we can deal with them as they arise."

"How much," Neil asked, "did you guess?"

"Nothing whatsoever. How can you, of all people," James demanded, "ask that?" He paused. "I don't remember much about those few seconds," he went on slowly. "What exactly did I do when I came round that last bend of the swimming pool?"

"You did what every other man in the circumstances would have done—you saw red," Neil told him. "You went crazy; you went beserk because you saw me—as you thought—holding Alison under the water. I wasn't holding her under; I was pulling her out—but you couldn't know that. All you realised was the necessity of stopping me, and as you were still some distance away, you picked up a stone and threw it straight at me. Too straight. It hit my forehead; it didn't knock me out, but it didn't leave me in good enough shape to fend you off when you reached me and began to use your fists. While we fought, I shouted. I shouted Eden's name and I shouted that I had seen him making an attempt on Alison's life, and I tried to tell you that I had hit him and he had gone under and I hadn't seen him come up. I shouted all that to you, but you didn't hear and perhaps you wouldn't have cared anyway. We fought and Eden died. If you hadn't come along, I would have got him out—but God knows what I would have got him out for. He'd reached another kind of end."

He paused, picked up the little elephant, studied it blindly and put it down again.

"Neil—" I said suddenly.

He didn't turn.

"Why, why, *why?*" I asked desperately.

"Hate." His voice was dull. "Hatred, and jealousy, and the fact that he could never bear being beaten." He turned slowly to face me. "You'd better know that I killed him. I killed him just as surely as if I'd held him under the water until he died, as he was trying to hold you."

"You were unconscious," James said. "How could you have told us he was down there?"

"That was at the end," Neil said. "The beginning was in Scotland on the day I walked across the fields to see Margaret and Eden, thinking as I went, that people sometimes got what they deserved: the small, sharp-tongued little girl had grown up and was to marry Eden and get what was coming to her.

"I was Eden's friend; his only friend. Even when we were at school, I recognised his potentialities as an actor; even when we were at school, he realised what I could do to de-

217

velop them. He had greatness in him—as an actor; as I'm no moralist, it didn't seem to matter much what he was like in other ways. It didn't matter to me one way or the other ... until the day I opened the door of the library and saw Alison sitting in the firelight."

He paused. His next words were addressed to me.

"You looked so beautiful, that for the first few moments I found it difficult to focus anything else in the room. And then I saw, sitting beside you, Eden—and what happened to me then is something it isn't easy to talk about, and impossible to explain. I went into the room and I suppose I spoke and behaved normally enough, but you were everywhere I looked. The thought that you were to marry a man like Eden sent the blood to my head. When I left the house, I was thinking of only one thing: how to prevent it.

"It was very easy. When you know a man as I knew Eden, you've got a lot to work on: his greed, his vanity, his ambition. All I had to do was express surprise that a man with his looks, with his charm, with his abilities, was to tie himself to a girl without money and without influence. I had no idea in the world—how could I have?—that Margaret was in love with him; she hadn't been home more than ten days. I'd forgotten how potent a spell Eden could put on all women. I didn't think at all of Margaret. I only thought of Alison. At least, that's what I told myself. During that walk from her house to my own, I sowed a seed in Eden's mind and it took strong root. Before long, I learned that Margaret and Eden were to be married, that Alison had left home and had sent no word and that her godmother's heart was all but broken. From that point to the moment when we looked down to see Eden's body in the pool wasn't a very long road.

"I left Edinburgh and I didn't see Eden again until he came to London to play the lead in *Fairground*. He told me three things in swift succession: that he'd married Margaret for her money and regretted it; that she had gone up to Scotland because she didn't feel she could face Alison—and that he was certain he could get back any ground he'd lost with Alison—if he'd lost any ground. I told him that if he went near Alison, I'd throw him out of the cast.

"I told you that it was his last chance. He knew only too well that his future depended on me. I was the only man who'd risk using him in an important part. You've got to bear that fact in mind, because it explains everything that comes later."

"When did you begin to smell danger?" James asked.

"Too late."

"When those banisters broke—" James paused.

"No. I had absolutely no suspicion. It would have been too fantastic, too much like a bad play. It wasn't until old Thomas at the Eagle Hotel showed me the damage to the brakes of Madame's car that the red light went up in my brain. I wasn't piecing things together, but I was beginning to remember things about Eden that made me realise he couldn't be ruled out of any mischief at any level. But I couldn't believe that he would want to harm Alison.

"And then the drunk old man died, and I learned from Alison that she had been standing beside him a few minutes before his death. I think that I knew then—but there seemed no sense in any of it.

"That night, at the Netherheath Inn, I decided to talk to Margaret. All I had in mind was getting out of her, without arousing her suspicions, Eden's feelings towards Alison. Before I had said very much Margaret had said a great deal. She told me that the reason she had turned up so unexpectedly in London was that while she had been at home, her mother had told her that she had changed her Will; instead of leaving Alison the sum of money that, as her godmother, she had bequeathed her, she had—on hearing from Alison again—decided to divide everything equally between Margaret and Alison. She didn't need to ask what Margaret felt about this. Margaret was so happy that she changed her mind and came to London to tell Eden the news and let him share her pleasure.

"When she told him, he told her, quite brutally that he had married her for her money and wasn't ready to dance at the thought of losing half of it. He went on to say that it was to prevent this very possibility that he had gone to the trouble of suppressing Alison's letters to her godmother.

"Margaret wanted to leave him at once—but there was more than his marriage at stake. She decided at least to wait until the play ended its run.

"While I was listening to her, I was remembering something: that Eden had come into the study one day and seen

Alison in my arms. I was absolutely certain that he decided, then and there, that my reason for dissuading him from marrying Alison had been because I was in love with her myself. It would tie up, in his mind, with my threat to get rid of him if he went near Alison in London."

He paused. James gave him a cigarette and he lit it with shaking fingers.

"I can write the next paragraph for you," James said. "He'd lost half the dowry, he'd lost Alison—and he realised he couldn't charm Alison back again. He'd have enjoyed killing you, but you were the goose that laid the golden theatrical eggs. You had to stay alive and well—but he could get his own back on you by making sure you'd never get Alison—and he could ensure, on the side, that Alison wouldn't get the money. Now you can go on."

"I saw Eden coming out of the gun room at Lord Weaver's house. He didn't see me. I went in and found that the rifle had been fired—but out of the window I saw, thank God, that Alison was safe. When I saw you with her, when you joined us and said that you were going to take Alison with you in your car, I guessed that you were on to something. When you didn't come back that night, I was sure of it. After that, I knew that it was a matter for the police—but where was the proof? What kind of story would I—or you—have had to tell?"

"You must have known he'd try again," James said.

"Yes. But how, when, where?"

"A swimming pool," James said reflectively, "isn't a bad
221

place for a good try; didn't you think of that?"

"No. I didn't. Alison was a first-class swimmer; Eden, in the water, couldn't touch her—so I thought. Besides, all of us were there; what could happen? When I went to change, he was with me; I saw him go into his room. When I'd got into my clothes, I went to look for him. He wasn't there. I didn't stop to think. I just moved—back to the pool…

We sat on in silence. We heard at last heavy footsteps marching along the corridor and I recognised Madame's tread. She knocked loudly on the door and James got up and let her in. She looked shaken, but it was clear that she was enjoying the importance with which the tragedy had invested her; her lamentations and clumsy comments on Eden's end were interspersed with spirited accounts of how the guests were reacting. She was, for the moment, the centre of attraction and, to my relief, could not give us very much of her time.

When she had gone, I went back to Margaret's room. She was awake. I stayed with her until she had fallen asleep. As I sat watching her, I heard a scratch at the door; it opened to admit James. He tiptoed across the room to me, sat wearily on the floor beside me and laid his head on my lap, and presently I realised that I had two sleepers to watch.

Chapter Thirteen

Neil and James did what they could to shield Margaret from the more difficult sessions with police and Press, but there was still much that she had to undergo. For the first time, we had cause to be grateful to Madame, who was only too eager to answer questions. She built up for the reporters a full though largely inaccurate picture of Eden's career and the brilliant future that was to have been his; we were to wonder always how much of the play's subsequent success came from the publicity that Eden, in dying, had given us.

He had died twelve miles from the town in which he had been born. He had no close relatives. His coffin was followed to the quiet little cemetery only by Neil and James, Margaret, Madame and myself and some sympathisers from the hotel. When the funeral was over, nothing remained but to finish our journey. Edinburgh lay ahead, but Eden would remain for ever in his lonely grave within the tall white walls of the cemetery.

The problem of a chauffeur for Madame's car presented some difficulties. Neil, it was clear, intended to drive Margaret home in the car that we had called Eden's but which was in fact her own. James was determined that I should travel with him.

The problem was solved by Madame herself; she had agreed, she told us, to give a lift to three reporters who were going North to cover the Festival; one of them would act as chauffeur. We saw her off, happy and excited in a kilt of Maclean tartan and a woollen tam-o'- shanter.

Neil had made himself responsible for clearing up Eden's effects; the two suitcases were placed, neatly packed, in his own room and he called James and myself in to ask whether we would take them up with us to Edinburgh.

"Margaret'll have to go through all the things," he said "but not now; not yet. For the moment, I'd rather keep them out of her way."

"I'll take them," James said.

"Thanks." Neil looked at us and then spoke quietly. "And that's all," he said.

His eyes went round the room in a blank, unseeing stare. They rested on the suitcases and, after a moment, he stepped forward and picked one up. James took the other and glanced briefly in my direction.

"Not quite all. Alison and I are going to be married."

"So much," Neil said, "jumps to the eye. Make her happy."

James looked a little surprised.

"Naturally," he said. "But what you can do from now on, is to stop looking backwards and keep your eye on what I can prophesy is a nice rosy future. I don't expect you to feel up to much at this moment, but I do know and I do point out to you

224

as a warning, that Scots sometimes tend to imagine that it's their own personal responsibility to uphold the nation's reputation for dourness. Melancholy can run away with you as it did with that Hamlet chap. And now let's close that book."

He opened the door and I went out. The two men, with Eden's two suitcases, followed me.

When I asked James two hours later to stop the car, he did so, and turned to look at me in surprise.

"You can't want to get out again," he protested "I let you out only ten minutes ago and—"

"I don't want to get out," I said.

"Then what? It isn't dawn. You can't want to haul up a flag."

"It's the Border," I said, "and I do want to haul up a flag."

"I see. Well, what do I have to do? Recite a poem by Burns?"

"What you do, you do only in the mind," I told him. "What you do is to drive on remembering that soon you'll be on ground historic and hallowed, where—"

"—men are Scotsmen?"

"Yes."

"I'll do my best. Do I have to be married in a kilt?"

"No. Now you may drive on."

"First," James said, "I have to point a moral. If Neil had—"

"The book's closed; you said so yourself."

"Only one last thing: when he saw you in that firelight and

got knocked off his feet, he wasn't thinking of saving you from Eden; he was only planning, sub-consciously, to save you for himself. So Eden was right."

"Where's the moral?" I wanted to know.

"I've just told you. If Neil—"

"You're havering." I said.

"I'm—? Oh yes, I see what you mean. Alison, ma ain lassie, do ye doot ma affection?"

"No, only your sanity." I pointed to the road ahead. "Home, James."

"There's no hurry," he said.

He took me in his arms and turned my face to his.

"Alison—"

He stopped, consternation overspreading his features. Abruptly, he released me and started the car. But instead of going on, he turned in a wide circle and drove rapidly southward.

"What in the—" I began, and stopped.

"I had it in my hand," he explained apologetically. "I just hung it for a moment over the counter when I paid the bill at the cafe we stopped at, and—" Panic crept into his voice. "You don't suppose anybody would have stolen it, do you?"

"No," I said hopelessly. "I don't suppose."

THE END

Consider the Lilies

by

Elizabeth Cadell

There was another, and a much stronger reason why Kathryn disliked the walk along the short cut. The lane went past the deserted stables of Crossways House, at one point crossing the wide, old, cobbled stable yard.

The buildings were rotting, and were half-hidden by creepers; the place had a desolate, haunted look and Kathryn found it so strangely frightening that there were times when she preferred to walk to the village the long way round—a proceeding manifestly absurd, she told herself angrily. She was not usually nervous, and could find no reason for her fear of passing the stables, but nothing could overcome the fear. The first part of the walk did not trouble her, for she could look back over her shoulder and see her own pleasant house; then the path curved sharply and on one side were the deserted stables, while on the other, separated by a low wall from the right-of-way, lay the old part of the churchyard, with its forgotten, sunken graves. Beyond the stables could be glimpsed the back windows of Crossways House; beyond the gravestones stood the Church and the Vicarage, but even these evidences of habitation failed to reassure Kathryn; she hurried along, humming or whistling her way past the worst part, hating herself for her foolishness; then the path, curving once more, shut out the gloomy picture and became a pleasant walk. Her fear was the more inexplicable because to the children, to her husband and to her two servants, the path was simply a short cut through the stables: quick and convenient, coming out as it did almost at the Church door. Nobody—not even Caroline—shared Kathryn's odd qualms.

Now she made no reply to Mrs. Lauder, beyond a nod meant to indicate that she would observe the ban on wheeled traffic. She had allowed Dandy to bicycle only as a sort of test case; if Mrs. Lauder had overlooked it, she herself would have bicycled along the path and there would not have been time to indulge in fears and fancies. Now the hope was quenched and she would have to continue to walk.

The disappointment drove from her mind her intention of leading up tactfully to the subject of the lilies. She turned to look out at them, and Mrs. Lauder's eyes rested on her with a spiteful look.

"Mrs. Lauder"—Kathryn turned to face her—"I wonder whether you would—"

"No," broke in Mrs. Lauder flatly. "No, I won't. You're going to say will I give the lilies to the Church for Easter; well, the answer is that I won't. I'm not a church-goer, and I never was, and if I were, I wouldn't go into any Church run by that useless, wander-witted Vicar." She raised a claw-like hand and pointed to the garden. "Those lilies are all I've got to look at, and I like them; they're going to stay there until they die. Some of them will go to old Mrs. Turk, because they'll do more good there than they will in Church; they'll cheer up a poor old deaf and dumb creature instead of a Vicar that makes far too much use of his tongue. Tell him to whistle for the lilies; he's never done anything for me and he's not going to fill his Church with my flowers. If he wants lilies, let him grow 'em." She raised a stick and thumped it on the ground, and the maid came in. "You can go out and get some lilies for old Mrs. Turk," she told her.

❧

End of preview.

To continue reading, look for the book entitled "Consider the Lilies" by Elizabeth Cadell.

About the Author

Elizabeth Vandyke was born in British India at the beginning of the 20th century. She married a young Scotsman and became Elizabeth Cadell, remaining in India until the illness and death of her much-loved husband found her in England, with a son and a daughter to bring up, at the beginning of World War 2. At the end of the war she published her first book, a light-hearted depiction of the family life she loved. Humour and optimism conquered sorrow and widowhood, and the many books she wrote won her a wide public, besides enabling her to educate her children (her son joined the British Navy and became an Admiral), and allowing her to travel, which she loved. Spain, France and Portugal provide a background to many of her books, although England and India were not forgotten. She finally settled in Portugal, where her married daughter still lives, and died when well into her 80s, much missed by her 7 grandchildren, who had all benefitted from her humour, wisdom and gentle teaching. British India is now only a memory, and the quiet English village life that Elizabeth Cadell wrote about has changed a great deal, but her vivid characters, their love affairs and the tears and laughter they provoke, still attract many readers, young and not-so-young, in this twenty-first century. Reprinting these books will please her fans and it is hoped will win her new ones.

Also by Elizabeth Cadell

My Dear Aunt Flora
Fishy, Said the Admiral
River Lodge
Family Gathering
Iris in Winter
Sun in the Morning
The Greenwood Shady
The Frenchman & the Lady
Men & Angels
Journey's Eve
Spring Green
The Gentlemen Go By
The Cuckoo in Spring
Money to Burn
The Lark Shall Sing
Consider The Lilies
The Blue Sky of Spring
Bridal Array
Shadow on the Water
Sugar Candy Cottage
The Green Empress
Alice Where Art Thou?
The Yellow Brick Road
Six Impossible Things
Honey For Tea
The Language of the Heart
Mixed Marriage

Letter to My Love
Death Among Friends
Be My Guest
Canary Yellow
The Fox From His Lair
The Corner Shop
The Stratton Story
The Golden Collar
The Past Tense of Love
The Friendly Air
Home for the Wedding
The Haymaker
Deck With Flowers
The Fledgling
Game in Diamonds
Parson's House
Round Dozen
Return Match
The Marrying Kind
Any Two Can Play
A Lion in the Way
Remains to be Seen
The Waiting Game
The Empty Nest
Out of the Rain
Death and Miss Dane

Afterword

Note: Elizabeth Cadell is a British author who wrote her books using the traditional British spelling. Therefore because these books are being published worldwide, the heirs have agreed to keep her books exactly as she wrote them and not change the spelling.

67747835R00130

Made in the USA
Columbia, SC
31 July 2019